THE LIAR KILLERS

THE

LIAR

KILLERS

BY ANFERNEE PARKER

THE LIAR KILLERS

This is a work of fiction. Names, characters, places, and incidents either are the product of the author's imagination or are used fictitiously. Any resemblance to actual persons, living or dead, events, or locales is entirely coincidental.

Book design by Stewart Williams
Edited by Julie Tibbott

ISBN 979-8-2183-4340-8 (paperback)
ISBN 979-8-2183-4341-5 (ebook)

www.anferneeparker.com

CHAPTER ONE

Cut Wrists

Strapped to a cold metal killing chair, a tall and lanky adult was straining to stay alive. Roger Aimes lay in that chair. Stiff as a board. Barely breathing. He knew remaining calm was key.

Stay calm… stay calm. Every time I get near these self-righteous pricks it feels like my head is going to explode.

One outburst and the honesty machine would slice his veins into crimson macaroni. His forearms reduced to bloody trailways as open as the mines he worked in. The X3 jig was attached tightly to both his wrists. He wasn't alone in the sanitary metallic room. A male figure in a white lab coat controlling the machine stood hunched over him, transparent control panel in hand.

"If you tell the truth with your statement, I'll let you go, Roger," grunted the scientist. He was in every way a Prelican—one of the supporters of Chancellor Prumpt's regime. Wearing the silver metallic tie with *The Restoration* Symbol embroidered in the middle. He tapped his foot rapidly against the floor while checking the time on his display.

How dare he speak so casually about the possibility of me being killed today? Ok, just accept the statement, accept it—don't deviate. If I deviate, I'll get sliced. If I reject and create a new one, three beeps and I die, hemorrhaging uncontrollably.

In the back corner of the room was a large white container filled with hydrogen peroxide. A quick and easy way to wash away the blood splatter when needed. Roger closed his eyes. He took a deep breath in, filling his lungs to capacity.

"I attended the mandatory community support meeting and listened to Chancellor Prumpt's agenda for the nation. I firmly support our leader, chosen by the people, and his resolve to uphold the ideals of the Restoration." Roger exhaled shakily. He couldn't stop his spine from trembling.

"PERIOD," Roger yelled.

Please let Marela's advice help, please… please.

He opened his eyes just enough to see the Prelican tiptoe behind the glass across the room, shielding him from any potential blowback. The machine started to buzz loudly.

One one thousand, two one thousand

Roger squuezed his eyes shut as the X3 jig let out an ear-piercing whistle.

Three one thousand, four—

CLINK

Sweat now dripped profusely down his forehead. He opened his eyes and looked down at his arms. The clamps had released him. His restraints followed at the touch of a button from the Prelican who reappeared in front of him. He massaged the deep grooves now molded into his wrists, as he stood up and walked toward the exit. Roger and the man in the lab coat never met eyes. He waited in front of the slider to be released.

The Prelican began reading from his handheld device.

"Thank you for participating in this exercise. Together we can all continue to make Novolica a great nation. In order to uphold the principles of the Restoration period, we all have pledged to build a nation of integrity and end mentirring for all eternity. May we all have peace, knowing that our leaders have no more authority than every citizen in Novolica. May we all have comfort, knowing that even Chancellor Prumpt is upheld to the standards created by the citizens of Novolica. Even our leaders agree to be tested by our most accurate and powerful Anti-mentir apparatuses at intervals of the people's choosing and no less than once a month. As we have fought for Novolica, we will do everything possible to remember her values."

He clicked a button on his screen, finally opening the entryway into the main corridor. Roger strode swiftly through the hallway, checking the time on his handheld.

At the front of the atrium a man was hovering in a chair behind the concierge desk. After noticing Roger, he shifted his finger sideways, moving the whole chair airily across the credenza to let him leave. The large slider rotated outward allowing Roger out into the breezy weather of the busy Finca city center.

There was commotion in all directions. Instinctively, he hurried north toward the magnetic railway cars that would carry him to the mine rows. Roger felt jittery from the feel of the magnetic clamps that had been cinched on his forearms. Near him were multiple dome-shaped wind bikes floating atop large circular air turbines. He trotted toward the shiloh station, zig zagging through citizens wearing brightly colored tracksuits. The passways were packed with street traveler devices propelling people lightly, crossing in all directions.

As he drew closer to the station, a large crowd came into view, moving away from the shilohs. Transparent screens from handhelds were flashing all around him with floating messages and virtual maps showing people where to go. Roger approached the gate and pulled his handheld from the pouch in the side of his shirt. He scanned himself through and jumped onto one of the lifter pads.

After a few seconds air pressure boosted him and a few dozen others to the platforms. The shiloh sliders opened, allowing the crowd to pile in. Roger maneuvered through the crowd to a seat in the back corner of the compartment.

After a few minutes of waiting, he heard the shiloh message activate, signaling the rail was about to start moving. Roger reached for his handheld device. The floating clock showed 11:15. He rolled his eyes.

It'll be another twenty minutes until I make it to the mine rows.

A sudden urge forced him back to his feet. He pressed through the commuters to the bathroom. He slid the handheld still clutched in his palm across the floating keypad to open another slider. A small doorway on his right lit up bright green and slowly opened as Roger entered to relieve himself.

Once inside a red light appeared behind him. After refastening his pants, he looked up at the mirror. He was still sweating. His rust-colored brown hair was damp. He never let it get long, but it was enough to rub against his forehead.

Roger grabbed one of the cloths to the left of the mirror and rubbed his head in a backward motion to shift his short hair toward his neckline. A bell rang as he selected the warm water setting on the spout in the basin in front of his thighs, which triggered a firm jet spray. Rinsing his face, he reached for another cloth to dry and wipe away globs of worry and moisture from his lime green eyes. His child-like face had no facial hair, fully exposing his long jawbones and squared chin. His chiseled cheekbones made him look malnourished. Roger reached down to flatten out his bright yellow T-shirt that read HYDROGEN ROW 15.

Though the work in the rows was not challenging, having to pump geothermal energy to provide cities with electricity could be very taxing over time. A very simple process that had been put into effect even before the Restoration, on a large scale once all the life killer energy sources had dried up across the nation.

"Someone paleeeeease get a move on will ya," Roger heard a voice whine.

The slider in front of Roger started to blink yellow. He rinsed his hands off and turned to exit the lavatory.

"Oh, what a citizen," cried the short anxious looking woman.

She then pushed him aside and waddled into the bathroom that had turned green again. Before he could get back to his seat, he heard a loud ding.

"Shiloh will be coming to a full halt momentarily. Please brace yourself and protect your handheld," a robotic sounding voice called out.

Roger quickly slid his handheld into the secure pouch in his shirt. He looked around for the nearest safety block and hurried to stand on it. The blocks were flat shapes carved into the floor and remained active to keep anyone from excess movement through magnetic force.

The newer shiloh cars moving within and between big cities like Leiton and Nationland had been calibrated to come to smoother stops as the 300+ kmh speeds brought powerful jerks. Unfortunately, the primary shilohs for travel in smaller towns like Finca and in La Bajo only had safety blocks. These shapes were altered to hold the same magnetic properties as what powers the shilohs. As soon as each transport started to decelerate, the platforms would generate equal force in the opposite direction of the citizen standing on it to stabilize their body and prevent movement.

Roger put his hand against his handheld and bent his knees slightly to prepare for the jolt. Leaving the transport, he could now see the bright metallic rows of the pumping systems bulging out of the terra. They were endless. The fields were behind a large, high tech warehouse where the largest supply of geothermal energy was produced.

As Roger approached the entrance to the warehouse, he felt his handheld jump in his shirt. He pulled it out and saw that Trisha had sent him an auto collect. Auto collect transmissions let the sender know the intended recipient was moving, even if they did not respond to the message. He had expected this note, as she always sent one on the days he was summoned into the Prelican base.

He scanned his handheld against the slider in the front of the warehouse. His work profile briefly appeared in the air. In large green letters, the word, "CONFIRMED" scrolled across the panel and at once, the slider opened.

Roger walked into the open courtyard to see hundreds of workers clustered together, chatting with one another. Some were wearing long sleeve, T-shirts labeled "HYDROGEN ROW '' similar to Roger's, with the corresponding number of their teams. Roger hustled over to his personal storage section. He swiped his handheld device over the scanner to open an almost completely empty shelf. He picked up his finger sheaths and slid them over his palms. He looked at the photos of him and his team from the row hanging in his locker.

"Rog… Hey Rog," someone called out to him.

Roger turned around to see Charly standing in the middle of a group of workers. "Bout damn time, brother. I see you got spared again. This man right here is untouchable, or like them Prelos would say—the most honest some bitch alive," Charly boomed with his loud announcer-style voice. "Did you try making one up today, Rog?"

Roger smiled and shook his head.

"Well hell, I don't blame you—I think my daddy was making his own statement when he got snipped back in '115. That was twenty-four years ago. Imagine how good them mah-jigs are now."

Roger sighed. Running into Charly while he was on one of his rants meant that he wouldn't start his workload till after the lunch break was over.

"He regretted every second of it I tell you." Charly glanced around at his rapt audience of coworkers. "He was a Restoration man, a fighter. He was there right alongside the first Prelicans starting the movement to make Novolica a garrrreat nation. Yessir, imagine being back-to-back with all of your closest buddies. You all join together to fight for something you's been told is all that matters. When you have a JOE that's real smooth with his words and got a silver tongue to charm a line of renegade bots into doing whatever he wants. We got to fix things, make the nation right again. And you know what… my daddy believed every word they were saying. When I was still wearing baby jumpers all he would tell me was they wanted to restore the nation. But then he got to thinking, what was they trying to REE-STORE it to? He started asking himself why he even did it in the first place and could never remember what was wrong about it for the life of 'em."

Roger moved closer to the group and jumped in before Charly made any more incendiary statements that could get him called in for an inquiry.

"Well Charly, we surely do appreciate you helping us to remember the great man your dad was. He probably fought with my grandpap in the Restoration. And none of us were there so all we can do is move forward now," said Roger calmingly.

The other miners all nodded in agreement.

Charly figured he had said enough and pulled his handheld from the pouch in his shirt under his left armpit. He projected the time for the entire group to take notice. 13:05. Without another word, the miners shuffled toward the back of the courtyard and into the fields. A few of them patted Roger on the shoulder as they left.

Charly turned to Roger. "Hey brother, before you head out—Sunny mentioned he wanted to talk to you earlier."

"Thanks, Charly."

As Charly turned to walk away, Roger noted his friend's appearance: large and round face with a bushy handlebar mustache: long, dark blond shoulder length hair that he always had tied up in a tight bun, and bushy blond eyebrows. Though Charly was shorter than most, he compensated for his height with enormous arms and bulging legs. The cover straps he wore over his mining shirt accentuated his muscles even more, but he never ceased to underestimate his own strength. His beady, dark brown eyes gave him a permanent look of scrutiny.

As he trotted to catch up with the rest of his team, Roger broke left to find Sunny. He walked toward the overlookers' dome that had a view of the entire mining area. When he saw Roger, Sunny's awkward half-smile widened as far as his partially frozen face would allow. Sunny was one of the directors of the mine. Everyone loved him and the effort he made to help all the miners learn and grow. Sunny made sure to take time to get to know each person that was a member of his team. He'd started out in the rows when he was seventeen which was technically illegal, but he found success nonetheless.

Sunny was one of the older directors, as most had been selected right out of universal education to take on the job. This is what made him unique. He had the experience to understand the ins and outs of producing geothermal energy like no one else. Without Sunny, many of the miners would not have been eligible to work in the rows, nor would they even want to for that matter.

Sunny was wearing a metallic tie with the Restoration symbol on the front. He wore tight green pants that were always mechanically buckled, with the director collared long-sleeve shirt and handheld pocket in front instead of its usual place near the rib cage.

"Hey Der Vroger, tanks fower comin' ovuh befow de shift. I'm vreally happy to see ya back buddy. Awe you feelin' OK?"

"Yah Sunny, thank you for the concern. Not my first time in there—even though you never quite get used to it."

Sunny smiled again with half of his lip and continued in his typical tongue-heavy tone, "De mentir jeegs affect us all vreally differentially, if you evoh need to take some time off, you juss let me know—we all awe a community togever heer."

Sunny reached out his hand and Roger quickly embraced him to savor the coaching moment.

"Thanks, Sunny," Roger beamed, feeling a lot better.

Sunny then pivoted on his left foot to turn around. After swinging his right foot full circle opposite his torso, highlighting his disability. With a newly ignited passion, Roger turned in the opposite direction and squeezed his hands together to activate his finger sheaths. The carbon protectors expanded to cover his hands fully as he trotted along to catch up with the team on row 15.

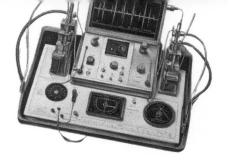

CHAPTER TWO

Life As We Know It

At the city center of Finca, far from the mine rows, were hundreds of connected housing pods. Because the living areas were powered by a shared source of geothermal energy, they were built close together to maximize efficiency. This made the housing developments look like large puzzles made up of interlocking cubes. In front of one particular pod read "420 GREEN MARSH LANE".

Roger Aimes sat inside with deep ridges still embedded into both his awkwardly placed forearms from his inquiry that morning. He had been waiting up, pretending to view the daily news on the hub when Marela de Nichols walked into their shared pod. Her long curly black hair was highlighted with mahogany streaks. Her wide, light brown eyes often overpowered her small triangular shaped face. As she approached, her blue dress swished side-to-side as she outstretched her arms toward Roger to casually embrace him.

Roger stood up from his resting cushion, expecting a long, drawn-out moment. Instead, only a half second after she had wrapped her arms around him, she had pulled back and walked toward the food storage area. He towered over Marela's small frame. He instinctively followed her toward the refreshments.

"Glad you made it back, Roger," said Marela nonchalantly.

"Yah, me too," he replied. "Your fix worked for me. I made sure to end the statement by saying period to straighten the… umm, what did you say that does again?"

Marela grabbed a large container that held her favorite kind of beans and started pouring them into a smaller bowl. She then reached for her salad as she faced him once again. "Ending your statement with certainty calms your breathing and allows you to feel more in contact with the statement on a neurological level. When you firmly say the word 'period', you inform not only the people around you, but also your brain that you truly mean what you are saying."

She mixed various food items into her beans.

"And you said that you and the team had figured this out with simulation testing of the X3's?"

"Not exactly. I was able to build a hypothesis of my own based on data files that were available about the machines' functioning."

She walked past him over to the sitting cushions in front of the hub and increased the decibels as she listened to every word being spoken on the daily notes.

"*Chancellor Prumpt has announced the date of his next public mentir screening, fulfilling his duty to honor the decree signed into law following the Restoration Movement. The Prelican Council reminds all citizens that you must report for screening upon being summoned.*"

The picture transitioned to a stubby looking figure with abnormally large hands and bright yellow hair draped across his forehead. He was fierce looking, with a permanently staunch facial expression. His bony arms poked through the jacket he wore. His neck jutted out beneath his wrinkled chin. His deep-set brown eyes were barely visible.

Chancellor Prumpt bellowed, "As part of the law, we are all required to maintain absolute integrity. We as a society have agreed to restore our once broken democracy by pledging our allegiance to this nation. We have fought earnestly to create a fair and equal society that is truly governed by the people. Citizens of Novolica, today is a great day." Roger grunted and turned away from the hub.

"So, tomorrow is a mid-week celebration. I made it through another screening. We should go find something to do after work," he said casually.

Marela kept looking at the hub as if he hadn't said anything.

"There's a new place in Haven district that has all types of pastimes. It may be worth visiting. I have a few plinkos saved up."

Marela half-turned toward Roger. "Those plinkos should be used toward your half of the rent. Besides, I've already made plans for tomorrow," she said, disinterested.

Roger looked down at the hairs on his arm and tried to think of something else to say, but nothing came to him.

Marela realized her comment sounded harsh and she smiled and looked at him squarely for the first time. "Though you making it back is something worth celebrating."

Roger looked back up at her briefly and felt a grin coming, but he held it in and nodded as he turned back toward the hub, listening to the live video feed.

"*Today in La Bajo, two citizens were cited for public display of misconduct. They were found spreading derogatory messaging against the nation's public servants.*

The hub's focus briefly glanced over the words drawn over a duct of the shiloh station: "Prelicans Kill The Integrity in—" As the message started to become smeared by a wipe crew, the focus moved back to the news commissioner.

"*They have been detained and their hearing scheduled for a later date to be determined.*"

"What do you think will happen to them?" asked Marela.

Roger could sense frustration in her voice as she spoke about government issues.

"They will be screened to test their loyalty to the Prelicans' rule. More than likely, their statements will be built around something that is sure to get them killed," said Roger. "You would think a nation ruled by its citizens would allow those people to express their views without threatening with their lives."

"You know this is how the Chancellor makes every day great for the citizens of Novolica," Roger said sarcastically.

Marela folded her arms over her chest and leaned back into the cushion. "Well, someone will step up and really restore Novolica one day."

Roger thought hard on what he could say to change the subject. He knew that Marela deeply despised the political climate of Novolica and had suffered serious personal losses because of it. Whenever these topics started to get to her, he always had the impulse to comfort her in some way.

"Do you want me to make some hot tooka? I could put some on the burner and add extra leaves… like how you used to—"

Marela sent him a silencing stare. "Roger, you don't have to do that for me," she whispered.

Roger wasn't convinced. He got up and walked toward the food storage area, looking for something to hold the herbs and warm the calming liquid. Marela slowly got up and followed him. She crossed her arms over her chest again and watched as Roger pulled the green pointed tips from a leafy plant. He crushed them together and poured steaming water over the leaves into a cup. After he added in another gooey white substance to make the mixture solidify, he pulled two spoons from the cupboard and handed one to Marela.

As they scooped out warm chunks of the tooka, she spoke in a dazed state. "Are you going to meet with Trisha tomorrow morning before heading to the mines?"

"Yea, it's best if I don't skip this time. Did you want to come along?"

"No, I have to be in early tomorrow for a new research project."

She finished her last scoop of tooka. Her eyes glazed over as she put her spoon in the e-wash and moved toward her bedroom at the opposite end of the pod.

She smiled at him. "Goodnight Roger, thank you for the tooka."

Roger watched her as she walked to her slider and it closed behind her.

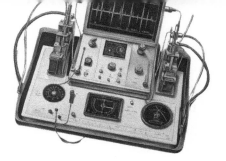

CHAPTER THREE

The Meetup

Sunlight peeked above the horizon and bright shimmers of light leaked into Roger's sleeping area. A loud buzz emanating from his handheld jerked him awake. He rolled over to the edge of his bed and silenced the device. After a lengthening stretch, he got to his feet and bobbed to the washroom. He attached his handheld to the play station and removed his clothes to bathe as soft music filled the space. He noticed that the ridges in his arm had finally started to fade. Once finished, he prepared food for his break at the mines today. As he was about to leave, he called out to Marela.

"Hey, I'm heading out. See you tonight." No answer. He moved toward her bedroom. "Marela, you there?" Still nothing. He approached her slider. "Marela, uhh morning. I'll see you later…yeah".

"Ok, be safe," she called back.

Roger stood frozen before turning to the main slider in the pod. He pulled his handheld out and took note of the time. He was earlier than usual and knew he would have plenty of time to get to Cafe Por Cafe to meet Trisha.

Roger headed out onto the passway away from his pod. He shuffled through people in the usual morning hustle and bustle. Citizens were crossing left and right, most eyes glued to their handhelds. The smell of clean air from recycling systems blew across the city. After the loss of eighty percent of the oxygen-producing plants, the best engineers in Novolica came together to create a new way for people to breathe clean air. After years of excessive contamination and children being born with birth defects due to lack of sufficient oxygen, the engineers had finally been able to create oxytanks. These large generators were now placed in cities all over the world.

Roger exited the residential neighborhood and passed one of the oxytanks before entering the city passway. He stepped casually alongside street travelers while dozens of wind bikes moved around him. He had a short distance until he arrived at the cafe. He wondered what his mother, Trisha would say to him about being summoned for a mentir test the day before. Their meetings after inquiries always went differently.

He looked to his right over the passway exit to an old sign that read "Cafe Po Caf". Both the "r" and the "e" had fallen off the mangy looking building sign. Roger approached the entrance to the dilapidated establishment. He didn't enjoy these older types of sliders that were sluggishly slow to open.

Roger walked in and found the familiar blue booth toward the end of the row. The woman sitting there had dark curly hair peppered with gray highlights and pulled up into a bun. She had tight skin and looked young for her age. Her square jaw and long face had a keen resemblance to Roger's. Draped around her neck was a bright green necklace that matched the green sleeveless dress she was wearing. She pulled out her handheld from a large purse to check the time when Roger stood in front of the table with a grin.

"Did you think I was going to be late?" Roger said smugly.

Trisha jumped to her feet and wrapped both arms around him. They sat down opposite one another as she began rambling excitedly.

"I still don't understand why you insist on getting these tops that have the handheld release at the rib. Isn't that uncomfortable?"

Roger sighed, "Nice to see you too, Ma. These shirts are better to keep the handheld functioning properly. When you throw it in your bag it could get all scratched up or even broken."

"We have been using pocketbooks for years and years to carry our devices without any issue, then someone goes and sews rectangular pockets all over shirts and pants—now all of a sudden, purses aren't safe. This world, I tell you."

"BAH ahaha," Roger laughed. "There is a lot more wrong with this world than how we carry our devices." He put his arm out on the table and pulled up his sleeve so Trisha could see the marks the X3 had left.

She looked at the indents on his skin and frowned. "Well, I am glad you told the truth. I don't like it either, but it is necessary. Before this, people were suffering from deceit all over. Someone could mentir as easy as buy a new handheld. We couldn't trust one another. Now I may have been young, but your grandfather told me all about how things were. He fought for the Prelicans because he knew that things needed to change. Jack Roger was a man who demanded respect. He wasn't afraid to speak his opinion and he was so tough. Ohh my father didn't care who he offended."

As Trisha gazed upward in a memory daze, she kept going on and on about her childhood and how happy she was that Roger was born after the Restoration War. Roger became uninterested and looked around for the WaitBot to order. As the small machine came around the corner from the back of the cafe Roger motioned his head in its direction to alert Trisha.

"I sure would love for the owners to get a few new bots around here," Trisha complained. "They must know they are starting to fall behind the times. Most places have ten or more bots circling endlessly to take care of patrons."

Roger turned smirking, "I have offered to meet you somewhere else over and over, but you love this place so much. Plus you always said that dad was good friends with the original owner."

Trisha leaned over to the bot to punch in her order into the screen showing on its front side.

"Yea, Blynt would claim that he was friends with the original owner, but who knows."

"ORDER ACCEPTED," the WaitBot chimed.

Trisha shrugged and looked in the distance toward the entryway slider. "I'm sure whomever originally owned this place is long gone, along with Blynt."

Roger was now more interested and wanted to remain on the topic, but he knew bringing up his father was sure to sour the mood.

He turned toward the WaitBot and spoke "One signature express with tint and one coddle muffin."

"MESSAGE RECEIVED...ORDER ACCEPTED."

The WaitBot rotated, showing the back panel of its small circular frame which opened up to reveal a row of glasses and a pitcher of water. Chilly air flowed from the compartment as Roger reached in and grabbed two of the glasses and filled them with water. Once the pitcher had been placed back into the WaitBot, the mechanism then rotated to the next booth.

Roger and his mother both sipped from their mugs. Trisha looked over to him excitedly as if a great idea had found its way into her mind.

"How is Marela?" she asked. "I am sure she was happy to see you back from your inquiry."

"She is the same as always. Still as negative as ever toward the Prelicans—"

Roger paused and looked around to see if anyone may have been listening to their conversation.

"She saved me... through her research, she concluded that certainty may inhibit a threatening response from the X3's. Even told me how to end my statement."

"Well, I don't agree with her trying to find ways to cheat our systems. But I am glad she told you what she knows. That woman still cares deeply for you, Roger."

Roger took a deep breath and looked down into his mug. "Yeah, well I can't—"

"I think it's time we convinced her that the way our Prelicans govern Novolica is what we all need. My daddy believed that this was the best thing that ever happened to Novolica. He gave his life for our citizens. Roger, you can change her mind... Live up to the name I gave you and fight for truth, like him."

Trisha's demeanor had gotten more serious, but she was careful to remain light in her words to avoid upsetting Roger by talking badly about Marela's views.

"Well, she certainly has her reasons, Ma. For all we know things have changed since Grandpap fought. Maybe he didn't know what would happen after the Prelicans took over. There's a lot of people you know... a LOT that don't make it through their inquiries. Do ya really think all those people mentir?"

Trisha let out a loud sigh. "You are seeing things so much differently these days, I remember when you were young and you wanted to be placed as an official of the state at the academy. You wanted so bad to meet the Chancellor in person." She forced a smile and gazed into her son's eyes. "I guess you have really become your own man."

The WaitBot returned with two trays on its outer shell. Roger quickly scooped up the large round pink-frosted pastry and handed the other tray to Trisha. She had gotten a small blue rectangular cake that was cut four ways.

"Do you want some morning hash?" she asked.

He reached over and scooped a piece of the cake onto his tray beside the coddle muffin.

As they ate, Roger asked, "Are you going to be at the range this week? I know last quarter you were upset you hadn't logged enough time to get the subsidy."

Trisha swallowed her last chunk of hash and nodded her head.

"I can buy you one of those new spine shields so it's not as painful to lay the seeding," Roger offered.

"No need, I don't plan on being there much longer—I can get by without the subsidy anyway. You would think forty years in a botany placement would be enough for the full support."

Roger sensed the frustration in her voice. He reached around the side of the booth to push the keypad and signal the WaitBot. Six minutes later it came rotating around the counter and back to them. Roger looked over the screen and scanned his handheld against the WaitBot's frame for the bill. It elevated above its normal height and scooped the trays off the table into its side compartment. Trisha grabbed her handbag and stood up beside the booth.

"I brought the wind bike today, do you want me to give you a lift to the shiloh station?"

"No, I will take the passway and be there in no time."

As they moved toward the slider Trisha reached up to pat her son on the back.

"Next week, same time. And try not to get called in again for a while," she said with a smile.

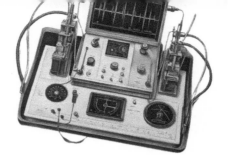

CHAPTER FOUR

Don't Say It

A woman emerged from the pod labeled 420 Green Marsh lane wearing loose blue jeans and a long sleeved white blouse, her long curly black hair with brown highlights waving behind her small framed face. In her left arm was a small duffle bag with her handheld in the opposite hand. She pressed two buttons on the device, causing a mid-model wind bike to whizz around the corner of the pods at the end of the row. It approached Marela, hovering above the ground.

Marela thought about when she first bought her wind bike eight years ago. The once bright white pearl shade had now turned into a dull beige. Despite its age, it still ran well and was able to hold a charge which made Marela happy to keep it. After the wind bike stopped in front of her, she walked around the back and slid her handheld across the slider access panel located near the bottom of the wind bike. A loud signal sounded and the shield protecting the vehicle rotated forward, revealing the driver seat in the middle of the bike and two passenger compartments on each side.

Marela sat her duffle bag in the one to her left and climbed up into the driver seat using the pedals behind each passenger compartment. She then straddled the driver frame and placed her handheld horizontally in a docking station in the middle of the control panel. She grabbed the two handlebars and as soon as she was in place, the slider moved backward, covering her fully within the vehicle. Once the shield had clicked in place, her hand rotated the throttle and immediately she whizzed off alongside the passway away from the residential pods.

As the wind bike approached the main intersection onto the expressway, Marela leaned her body to the left, shifting the driver seat downward and maneuvering rapidly through traffic. Despite her jerking body movements and the driver section of the wind bike leaning with her, the duffle bag and the two passenger seats on both sides of her remained perfectly still. She glanced down at the control panel showing current precipitation, air quality, traffic levels, charge level of the wind bike, and a small yellow area that was showing her the path to get to the factory in Leiton City. Her estimated time of arrival showed how many km were left. Accelerating would calculate how fast she would need to go continually to reach the factory by her preferred time of arrival. Since Marela kept every location and arrival time on her handheld, the wind bike's control panel could show it.

Beside the throttle was a small yellow square switch labeled "Auto Engage". With a flick of her thumb, Marela had activated the mechanism and placed her feet on the step rests adjacent to the passenger seats to lift herself out of the driver seat. She stepped over into the passenger side and moved the control panel access to the left screen. As she slid down into the deeply positioned passenger seat, she scrolled across hub screens similar to the one she looked over at the pod.

One title read *Today's News Update- April 16th 2129*. She had to restrain herself from selecting it.

She flicked her hand to the left, swiping away the hub channels and showing her personal favorites. She clicked "music" and selected "mix" from the long list. The speakers in the side panels, on the edge of the slider and under the control panel in the driver's seat began to reverberate. Deep bass from her favorite music vibrated the entire wind bike. She felt surrounded by the bells and electric hand claps in between the long drawn-out soft wails of a lightly singing woman. Bobbing her head side to side, lifting her shoulders up and down, Marela mimicked the mechanically placed beeps and cymbals of the music. Feeling satisfied and enthusiastic about the day, she passed the control panel back to the driver screen and stood up to mount the driver seat. She gripped the throttle, deactivating auto engage and pressed "Slider Reveal". The shield that was protecting the inside of the wind bike moved outward in a circular motion, allowing the air from outside to whoosh into the interior of the vehicle. Marela's hair fluttered wildly behind her.

She reached through the floating display and grabbed her eyewear from a hidden compartment. The control panel now projected through the black auto-specs in front of her face. An AI generated path through traffic now guided her. Marela squeezed her right hand tighter around the accelerator and pulled back hard with her wrist, flexing her knuckles upward. The wind bike zoomed forward. The auto spec display shifted to a wide view angle of the entire expressway in Marela's path. She could now see how to maneuver to avoid collisions. The AI system auto control assisted her in rapid weaving around obstacles.

A small red dot appeared in the top right corner of her display that read "Leiton City". The wind bike locked on and veered right off the expressway. As the dot on the auto specs grew larger, Marela slowed down and relaxed her body that had been hunched tightly over the driver seat. In the city, there were stricter rules on the maximum speed allowed. She wanted to avoid her wind bike locking up and shutting down for thirty minutes which would be the consequence of breaking the speed mandates within the city.

Marela sat completely upright now and took off the auto specs. The electronic dashboard reappeared in front of her. She enabled the top slider covering the wind bike once again, dimming the bright sun and cutting off the wind. She engaged the autopilot again and reached for her duffle bag. Marela placed her thumb on the scanner at the front end of the lining. The metallic strip on top of the bag turned green, allowing her to open it. She grabbed a blue brush. She adjusted the setting on the back causing a white light to emanate through the front of the handle in an arc. She placed the arc on top of her disheveled hair that had been ravaged by the blowing winds.

She rocked sharply to the left trying to steady herself as the wind bike made a turn and approached a large sign that read "TRN Inc". She hovered the blue handle down and back, down and back, and back forward along her long brown streaked hair. It was transformed from a tangled mess to its normal, flattened wavy texture. She activated the mirror on the wind bike's control panel and examined the effects. Marela forced a smile into the control panel's mirror mode, then clicked the brush handle off and stuffed it back into her duffle.

The wind bike had now come to a complete stop beside the factory. Marela took back control of the vehicle and maneuvered to the "Stationment" area. After her wind bike had been stored and locked, Marela hustled toward the entrance of the factory.

"Well good morning to you too missy," shouted a voice from behind.

Marela slowed down and turned toward the excited lady strutting to catch up with her.

"Oh, hi Jessa," she said warmly to her coworker as they both headed toward the large slider.

Jessa was a tall slender woman. Her yellow blazer was paired with a form fitting blue skirt. Her heels clicked loudly as her elegant, dangling earrings flashed brightly. Her half shaved red hair was tucked neatly behind her left ear revealing heavy eyeliner and shadow.

There were workers pouring in all around them. Men and women both young and old. TRN employed a little over a thousand citizens to build mentir detecting machines. A few hundred employees worked in the marketing and public relations departments to handle all publicity associated with X-series machines and new releases. There were another 400 staff members working the assembly lines to put together each jig. The work areas that had the fewest employees were reserved for the best and brightest engineers. These were departments like Machine Logic for accuracy testing; Machine Design for optimal results, Research and Development for future models; and Data Analysis where Marela worked.

Each area was segmented by type of mentir detector. Marela's segment focused on Class 3 citizens and below which included herself and Roger. The next segment above her focused on Class 4 citizens like director level workers, and city representatives. The smallest segment in the entire factory which employed less than ten individuals was focused on the development and implementation of Class 5 citizen level mentir detectors.

These jigs were only used for the Chancellor, his cabinet, and high-ranking officials. Since the Class 5 positions were the most important to keeping Novolica safe and truthful, citizens at this level were required to be screened for mentir testing publicly every month with X5 Mentir Machines that were known as the most accurate and highly likely to detect any trace of deceit, chicanery, or dishonesty.

Once Marela and Jessa had crossed the large slider entrance, they were corralled into single file lines and required to use their handhelds to identify themselves to enter the facility. Large scanners standing straight up at eye level verified each handheld and then did a facial detection of each person holding the device to ensure a match.

The factory was massive, with long corridors in every direction. Marela had worked there for the past eight years, yet not seen a third of the areas inside the building.

As soon as they passed the security checkpoints, Jessa said "Shall we go and grab drinks? I need a quick pick-me-up before we go to the lab."

Marela contemplated Jessa's offer as she moved toward the East Wing.

After a few seconds she looked up at Jessa and said sternly "Thanks, but I'm going to go ahead and head up I'll see ya there."

Marela hustled to the lifters. Once she reached the end of the first floor East Wing building, she pulled her handheld from her bag. She swiped it across a panel in front of the cylindrical glass tubes that were vertically transporting employees to the upper levels and a thick round metal platform appeared in front of her feet within the tube.

She stepped onto the platform and watched a small slider close behind her. The lifter hoisted her up to her designated floor. Bright yellow numbers displayed in front of her: 3…. 4….. 5…...6……..7.

"EMPLOYEE 721 De Nichols, Marela- LEVEL 7 ENGINEER", a robotic voice echoed.

A loud DING sounded and the slider opened. She walked out into the hallway and entered a room labeled "CLEAN" a few steps away. In the clean room there were a few other engineers in her department getting ready to start their long and arduous workday.

Ross was the first to greet her while he was pulling on his lab coat. He was the nicest worker on the team and always went out of his way to make sure everyone else was having a pleasant day. He was the most senior engineer and had been working in Class 3 Data Analysis for twenty-nine years.

"How'rya feeling this morning Marela? Did you open up the wind bike today? It sure is good weather for it."

Marela stuffed her duffle bag into one of the compartments and reached for her lab coat. She looked over at Ross and forced a half smile. "Sure did, Ross."

She proceeded to greet everyone else still in the clean room to end the conversation with Ross as soon as possible.

"Aaron, Emily, Jen, good to see everyone."

Ross noticed her hesitancy. He closed his compartment and tucked his slider into the front pocket of his lab coat. He led Jen and Emily into another room connecting the clean room to the work area. After the slider had completely shut behind them, Aaron, who was sitting down in the back corner away from everyone else, turned toward Marela as he was pulling on his lab shoes.

"Haha, why do you have to be so mean to Ross, MD?"

Marela tied back her hair and without looking toward Aaron huffed loudly "He's always so…so upbeat and happy. There is nothing happy about what we do here."

"Bullshit, he reminds you of Briyano doesn't he?"

Marela winced and grabbed the left side of her chest. She slowly turned toward Aaron and scowled. Aaron pushed himself up from his knees, now standing with his palms facing forward and arms outstretched in front of him.

Aaron met Marela's eyes and could tell how furious his comment had made her. He looked down at the floor and apologized profusely.

"Look, I didn't mean to upset you. You and I both know this is a shit job. The money they pay us will never make up for the people whose lives are ended due to the data we collect."

Just then, Jessa burst into the room with her morning juice and greeted Aaron. Marela, who was still trying to collect herself quickly moved into the lab without responding.

"Marela, are you ok?" Jessa asked as she caught a glimpse of the ferocity on her face.

Once the entrance had shut behind her, Jessa turned toward Aaron.

"What the hell did you say to get her all riled up like that?"

He tried thinking of something else to lighten the mood and quickly changed the subject. "Which juice did you pick out today?"

Jessa put her cup down in front of her assigned compartment and walked toward Aaron. She came face to face with him and stared coldly into his chubby face. Her tall, slender frame towered over Aaron and she glared down at him. After a few moments of extreme silence Aaron crumbled.

"Look, I may have mentioned Briyano to her after Ross went over his morning spiel with everyone. I didn't think it would get her all upset like that. I mean…it's been TWO YEARS. I was trying to make a point, that's all."

Jessa took a few steps back, almost losing her balance at the sound of the name of Marela's ex-fiance.

"You... how can you mention his name around her so casually?" she stammered. "You have absolutely no class you... you JERK!"

"Look, I said I was sorry, no need for you to get all emotional on me too."

Aaron pulled his handheld from his compartment and moved it toward his mouth.

"JILO, remind me to send MD a gift after today's shift," he enunciated word by word to the small transparent device.

A female voice from the handheld said "CONFIRMED."

Aaron tucked the handheld back into the compartment. He got to his feet and headed for the work room. He avoided eye contact with Jessa, still feeling her piercing gaze on his back. Before he crossed the slider she threw one last desperate attempt to guilt him.

"Citizens with no respect or regard for other's emotional stability never make—"

Before Jessa could finish her sentence, Aaron had cleared the entryway and the slider had closed behind him.

Soon after changing and finishing her juice, Jessa followed the team into the workroom to begin data calculations. The work rooms on Level 7 were elaborate. Each team member had their own work area with a digitized workspace embedding a large see-through panel.

There was a smaller display beside each C-Panel used to call other departments, conduct meetings, or contact non-employees since handheld devices were not allowed. When TRN personnel had to change rooms or workspaces, they could remove their customized type-decks from the digital workspace slot sitting directly below the C-Panels. They could be re-inserted into any other workspace to transfer all of their work, credentials, and data. Without the employee type-decks controlling the C-Panels they would be useless invisible screens.

Around the testing and data generation area, Ross directed Jessa and Emily about a potential bug that had been discovered in one of the X-series programming after a recent update. Meanwhile, Aaron had volunteered to record data logs for Marela, something everyone dreaded doing. Working at TRN was considered a high quality and lucrative work assignment, but no one there was particularly motivated or happy about the work they were doing.

The general consensus amongst TRN employees was that their job was necessary and helped them contribute to society while paying well. Nonetheless, occasionally a worker would have an outburst or mental breakdown of some sort. These events often occurred at the end of each month when the number of citizens referred to mentir screenings increased.

The last employee who had an outburst worked in the promotions department. The rumor swirling around was that his daughter had been called in for a screening the week before and had tested positive for mentirring. She had been engaged and was scheduled for the uniting ceremony a month after the screening. Word also got around that her fiancée was the one who referred her to be screened. After this news had spread, the promotions department was tasked with spinning the story to encourage other couples to refer one another for screening so that everyone's ultimate truths were in alignment before committing to long term relationships.

Instead of giving the grieving employee the week off so this project would be completed without his knowledge, his superiors thought it would be best for him to lead the project since he directly benefited from this referral to screening. After he was briefed on the project, he went absolutely bananas. Throwing C-Panels and ripping up workspace wiring from the floor. His screams could be heard across his entire division. It took five security guards to finally restrain him and escort him from the building.

They tried to keep things under wraps. Unfortunately, the security footage showing the outburst was leaked onto DETUBE, a banned hubsite known for reporting news against the views of the Prelican Regime. The employee's badge and records were wiped and he was never heard from again. Marela was able to find a lightweb portal to gain access to the footage. According to her, it was worth the risk to know what was really going on.

~

"How did everything go today?" Roger asked Marela once they were at home later that evening.

Roger had a natural gift for the perception of other's feelings. He could tell that something was seriously bothering Marela today more than the normal politics and state of the nation issues she felt so strongly about. Marela looked up at him with a disgruntled face. She knew that mentioning Briyano was always a sensitive and painful topic for both her and Roger. The last thing she wanted was to cause more pain by hurting his feelings.

"Not good. I saw that there's a General Action and Consensus Renewal coming up soon. Thinking about it makes me feel awful."

"Why do you feel so off about it? The same result will come from it that has happened every time a renewal comes around for the past 40 years since the Restoration started."

"I really want things to be different. We need better leaders. Someone who will step up and fix everything the Prelicans have ruined for us."

Marela felt more centered now.

"Chancellor Prumpt is a power hungry dictator that doesn't care about anyone but himself. Novolica deserves a real commander, who is noble and brave enough to challenge the Chancellor during the General Action and Consensus Renewal. This is the only real opportunity anyone would ever have to save citizens' lives and give us true fairness."

"Let's be real M, no one would be able to convince enough people to vote against the Chancellor. We've had one for the past 40 years. No one has stepped up yet! Why will it be any different five months from now?"

"They would be a hero, that's why. It only takes one person to stand up and declare what so many of us have been thinking—including you Rog—that the Prelicans are toxic for the nation and all they have done is divide and spread distrust and hate amongst citizens to accomplish their own personal goals."

"This is such a waste of time!" His voice got louder. "Why give in to false hope and let this run your life so much? Face it, this is how things are. The best thing we can do is ONE, not piss anyone off to avoid citizen's inquiries, TWO don't trust anyone that supports Prelicans, and THREE, you keep finding ways to not get slashed when we do get screened. It is what it is."

Marela looked deeply into Roger's eyes and regretted her decision to not tell him the truth about why she was upset. She realized that all she wanted in this moment was to be consoled and not argued with. Marela lifted her chin up high to hold back her tears.

"It only takes one—one word to take away the one you love, a friend, a family member. We should be able to focus on better things, but we can't because of them."

Marela stood up and before Roger could say anything else, she quickly retreated to her sleeping area. She refused to let anyone see the tears raining down her narrow cheeks. Not even Roger if she could help it.

CHAPTER FIVE

Authority Unseen

Roger entered the mines the next day still thinking about his conversation with Marela. He barely noticed he had arrived at work an hour early. At his personal storage area he found himself nearly alone on the floor. Well, nothing wrong with getting started earlier he thought. He pulled on his finger sheaths and walked toward the row. On the way, someone caught sight of him. "Atta Boy, keep our numbers high!"

Roger turned to his left in shock. Johnson Deary rarely showed his face to the common mine workers. Roger recognized him from the management communications messages. The man walked toward Roger excitedly.

"What's your name, buddy?"

"Roger Aimes," he said while standing as upright as he could, showing his full height.

Roger reached out his hand for a formal greeting.

"Nice to meet you, Mr. Deary."

"Likewise. I'll tell you what, I've got some morning lix and a few coddle muffins in my office. Why don't you come up, I'd like to learn more about you, Roger."

These typically were the types of encounters Roger tried to avoid. The more people that know you increased your chances of being submitted for citizen's inquiries.

"Sure thing Mr. Deary, I've always wanted to try it, but elixir can be hard to find."

Roger remembered seeing some messaging on his handheld about elixir and all its different strains engineered to help with activities like working out, reading, or getting an energy boost in the morning. It cost 2500 plinkos a container. A year's worth of shiloh tickets.

Deary led Roger to the management towers of the row. They walked until they reached a metallic finished wall. Johnson removed his handheld from the slot on the inside of his jacket and swiped it in front of a small screen. A hidden slider then shifted on the wall revealing a blue lifter.

"Let's take her up," huffed Johnson excitedly.

Roger filed in behind him on the narrow lifter. Roger had seen many photos and advertisements of Johnson Deary since he had started working at the mine rows but couldn't help thinking how different he looked in person. Deary had dark blonde hair slicked backward. His hair gel had a very strong smell that was now filling Roger's nostrils since they had mounted the lifter together. He and Roger were almost the same height, though Deary had large bulging shoulders covering a short, almost unseen neckline. He wore a tightly fitting patterned jacket over top of a professional looking tunic. He was still holding his handheld upright when Roger noticed all the upgrades on this model—magnetic adhesive to stick to any surface and project video enabled calls onto large surfaces, 10x grade glass that would withstand being dropped into a GTE generator, and a hard key shell on its base that could be used to directly access multi-layered security barriers.

"We're almost there now, my floor's private so it takes a while for the lifter. You know, most people at your level never get to use this one," Deary said with a snicker.

As the lifter approached, a red hard key access panel lit up on the control pad. Roger realized why Johnson Deary hadn't put away his handheld yet. He slid it into the hard key access slot blinking on the lifter's control panel. The panel turned green and the slider opened outward, revealing an executive suite.

Roger was taken aback. This office was larger than his entire living pod. The room was filled with chrome plated tables and hover chairs centered around them. There was a massive food storage area and a beverage fountain with six different flavors of water and juices.

"HAAR-HAAR, it's a beauty isn't it?" responded Deary to Roger's look of amazement. "This way, my boy".

"Well…it certainly is nice up here. I can tell a lot of…thought was put into the design."

Hearing this had completely ballooned Deary's already massive ego.

"I'm glad you appreciate it. I had twenty architects come in to get the layout of the room right," Deary boasted. "I'm sure you would have noticed those fine details and made the same decision if put into my position—what did you say your name was again, son?"

"Roger… Roger Aimes," he responded while trying to mask his irritation.

"Aimes… Aimes—HELL, you're one of Sunny Jacks' workers. That's right, I've heard him call you out once or twice during our briefings as a standout in the mine rows."

This made Roger feel a lot better. He knew that Sunny thought highly of him, but never would he have thought he'd been giving him recognition to the directors.

"If Sunny says you're alright then you are good with me! One of our best down there, that Jacks. He may even take my place someday."

Roger and Deary arrived at the slider of the private office and once again Deary had to use the hard key shell of his handheld to activate it.

"Have a seat on one of the hover chairs. We still have about fifteen minutes before you need to be back at your post."

Roger eased into the one nearest to him, sliding downward into the thick floating cushion. The chair contoured to his body from the angling of his back to his arms naturally resting at his sides. He couldn't imagine how anyone had a productive meeting in one of these without falling asleep.

Deary grabbed two large coddle muffins from a storage unit under the table and slid one to Roger. Roger leaned forward and the chair followed, positioning him more upright and allowing him to grab the muffin off the table. He then settled back in the reclined position and picked away at the large blue snack.

"The lix is in the compartment in front of you. I think there's Morning Glory and Focused Attention left."

Roger opened the storage unit and grabbed the first small box of liquid he felt. Glancing over the description read: *Morning Glory, engineered to wake up your nervous system and release endorphins in an immediate effect.* He opened it, excited to try the famous concoction. As Deary watched Roger pick away at the food he had given him and sip the elixir, he looked as if he was trying to think of something meaningful to say.

"Personally, I'm glad to have you out there in the row, the work we do here is not only critical to the survival of Novolica, the more GTE we can produce, the more profitable our company remains. Believe me when I tell you, we have been on FIRE these past few months. We have produced way over our minimum quotas...and it's made people happy."

Roger sensed hesitation in his voice. He smiled at him and nodded. This relaxed Deary so he continued on, "Every individual like yourself Rog is making a difference down there. None of this would be possible without the work you all do day in and day out harvesting the energy. I think we'll want to bring in a few dozen more over the next couple of weeks to keep productivity high. We'll need determined workers like yourself to show the new ones the way and—"

Deary's handheld started to buzz and he pulled it from his jacket slit. As he glanced at the screen, his expression turned serious. Before answering the device, he straightened up and pulled his jacket tighter.

"Mr. Manford, to what do I owe the pleasure...sure thing, anytime you need to have a word I am available. First, how's the Big Guy doing…ok no problem Mr. Manford, what do you need? Yes sir, the company is doing great—profits are through the dome. We've seen productivity remain high and our margins couldn't be better. We actually—come again?"

Something had hit a nerve with Deary. He stood up defiantly.

"How do you expect me to—"

As he listened to the scathing news on the other end of the call he suddenly remembered that Roger was still in the office. He looked over to him and faked a smile, which actually came off as sort of a grimace. While still holding the handheld, he walked over to Roger and ushered him swiftly toward the slider.

Without telling the caller to hold or even saying a word to Roger, he sent him on his way back to the rows. He eventually made it back to the lifter and was taken to the ground floor. He walked back out in the common area where other workers were stowing things and putting on protective gear. Roger looked for a familiar face and finally spotted him, entertaining a group of workers.

"HEELLL, I don't know how we done it, but BOYS we are stridin' long and fast," Charly boomed. Deary Mines Incorporated has pumped 2500 megawatts of pure geothermal energy from this sucker. No mine row has seen production this high since Tyson engineered the Eco Booster. If we keep up this pace, we all likely to see some extra PLINKOS in our handhelds."

The people surrounding Charly nodded in agreement.

"We got Novolica all powered up and I bet Deary himself is up in his office right now figurin' how we're going to send some of this energy to EurAsia National or AfriKingdom. We all know where this shiloh's headin' no matter if you're a career assignee to the mine row or you're a transfer from another track, we all getting bonuses. We deserve it!"

The guys around Charly got to their feet with excitement.

"That's right, Charly!"

Roger saw Paco shout while pointing at Charly. He had started working at the mine around the same time Roger started. Paco was a career transfer so he was older than most of the workers there. Like all citizens of Novolica, he was required to work in his career specialization field that was decided for him when he was thirteen years old.

After finishing the specialized training up until age twenty, Paco followed the law and worked in culinary packaging and preparation for the minimum fifteen years. He had told Charly once who told Roger later he struggled to complete a successful transfer at first. He waited five years for the paperwork to get resolved but had quit his specialization while things worked themselves out.

He moved to La Bajo and had to find ways to take care of himself "outside of the system." Eight years ago he was finally reassigned to mine work and had been happy ever since. Paco was called in most for inquiries out of anyone Roger knew. He wondered if it had something to do with all the time spent being unregistered in La Bajo.

Other workers started to chant as well, rallying around Charly. Out of the corner of his eye, Charly noticed Sunny walking toward the group.

"Hey fellas, it's the head honcho! SUNNY, have you come bringin' us the good news?" Everyone made way for Sunny to approach. Sunny was smiling brightly showcasing, his perpetually happy disposition. Everyone had gotten quiet in preparation to hear what Sunny had to say. Now standing in the middle of everyone he paused.

His large half smile widened as he said, "I wud juss like to say tanks to awe of you fower shuch garate wok ovuh de past yea! De company hass been vreally sugg-seckful dis yea becaush of yaw hod wak," Sunny blasted enthusiastically. "Vwrokin at Deary Mines incopowerated hass been de bes time of my life becaush of you awe. I am lookeen' fohwad to vrowking wit each and eveerey one of you until I can't not stand up eny mow. And I am gowin to vrecomean my team fower de masheemum bonus payouts!"

Everyone clapped loudly. No one at the mines was more loved and respected than Sunny Jacks.

"Wef des fingur sheefs," Sunny raised his voice as high as he could while pulling a pair of work protectors from his long johns, waving them them above his head, "we vwok togesher ash one fameely, and get GEETEE-EE fow awe garate restowed nation."

With this final word, everyone surrounding Sunny pulled out their finger sheaths and headed towards the rows. Many of them stopped to shake Sunny's hand or give him a pat on the back before leaving.

Charly caught up to Roger and patted him firmly on the back. "Man, are things looking GOOD for us. You heard what Sunny said? The maximum bonus... I can finally buy a wind bike for my daughter to get to her classes. Taking the shilohs makes it harder for her to put her schedule like she wants it."

Charly looked at Roger with a sly smile as he pulled on both his finger sheaths.

"What're you going to do with all them extra plinkos? Buy something for Marela I bet."

Roger turned away after hearing this, though he couldn't hide the smile that had peeked through. Charly figured he'd had his answer.

"I met Johnson Deary this morning, because I had gotten in so early—I ran into him walking the bottom level."

"No shit!"

Charly leaned hard onto the levers at their posts on the rows.

"Yea, he showed me up to his office and everything. We started talking and he said how much he liked Sunny too. Right before he got some important call and booted me outta there."

"Must have been some call, a man like him probably never has to answer to nobody—he could have sent them to auto-voice if he wanted. What would they say?"

"Yea, but he did answer it and he lost his nerve against whoever it was he was talking to. He started going on about the company's earnings and all. Then it sort of seemed like they were going to force him to do something. He started arguing back—and that's when I left."

Roger grabbed the long metal rod fastened onto a large round chrome dome in the ground and started to shift it back and forth.

Across the rows, a few other workers were mirroring the same motions at their stations. The combined force would activate the water pumping process, pushing it deep into the ground.

The more people they had pumping, the faster they could generate the necessary supply to heat up the turbines and produce more energy. They all worked in tandem, tirelessly day in and out. Their work was steady and simple. It didn't require them to risk their lives on the job or by inquiries from management. They were a tight knit family and there were never any arguments or conflict amongst the workers.

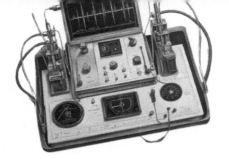

CHAPTER SIX

Inebriated Fairness

All of the workers in the mine rows would break at 1100 hours together to eat and return to work at 1300 hours. By 1800 hours everyone would leave. Around 1750 hours, Roger was gathering his things from personal storage when Charly approached him from behind.

"Rog, whadya say we grab a drink before you head home?"

Roger shrugged. "Yea, sure thing. Where'd you have in mind?"

"I'm thinking we go over to White Rose," Charly said, leaning onto Roger's shoulder as they headed for the exit.

Although Charly's smaller height forced him to stretch to reach Roger's shoulder, his stocky build almost tipped him over completely. This man should not have been shaped the way he was. Though he used his muscle and framework to his advantage.

"The White Rose is a dodgy shack, man," Roger moaned.

They had been there numerous times before and he had never really enjoyed the experience. They walked toward the nearest shiloh station as Charly continued to ignore Roger's pleas to pick somewhere else. Charly glanced over the signs to ensure they were boarding the correct one.

"Here we go, Rog—C7 takin' us de-rectly to Centro Finca."

Both of them pulled out their handhelds and swiped them as they entered the floating transportation cart. The compartment was filled to max capacity. People all around them were leaning against the walls, sitting on all the props, and covering all the safety blocks. Roger and Charly barely squeezed inside and scurried for parts of safety blocks to prevent being knocked backward by the magnetic force of the shiloh. Charly looked over toward Roger, annoyed of how tightly they were packed for this trip.

"Lucky we are only two stops away," said Roger reassuringly. He looked up at the display floating above their heads.

The station they would be stopping at showed an arrival time of eight minutes. Before that the guide showed a location highlighted called Nondol and another listed as Foxite.

"Centro Finca would be a two minute trip if we had ourselves a nice power glider. I'm still saving up—then there would be no need to keep waiting for these crammed shilohs."

One of the passengers standing beside Charly turned and looked at him scowling.

"Why do YOU need a power glider?" she said sarcastically in a high pitched voice. "You will only be traveling from the mines and whatever dusty old pod you reside in until you become a retro. No need to waste any helium on you."

Charly looked astounded. Before he could say anything to scold the woman Roger cut in. He looked at her squarely in the eyes and said in a bold voice, "How we get placed and where we live has nothing to do with what we can own or who we are."

The lady turned squarely on Roger and called out, "I don't need to know who ya are—a bunch of Class 3's like the rest of us on this shiloh. You and me both will be on here until we're 78, or unless you have a bad inquiry. Looking at your friend here I'm sure he'll have plenty of opportunities to take the shortcut," she said gesturing toward Charly.

Ignoring the woman's comment, Charly looked up at the floating display that now had "Foxite" highlighted in big letters.

"We're outta here, Rog," Charly said in a deeper than usual grunt as he walked toward the shiloh slider that had swiveled open.

Roger took one last glance at the sour woman. She looked ready to keep talking. However before saying anything else, Roger had swept through the exit to the outside.

"I have'n eeven been called in for no inquiry in close tuh year now. She ain't got a clue—probably feelin' all sideways cause of how she got placed as a starter. That ain't our fault. Nothin better than mine work in my book. Class 3's get the best deal—all that stress of havin to get an inquiry every six months to call yurself a city official or somebody's boss. Class 4's hardly make it more than two or three years without getting cut. Remember the last bloke before Deary started running the ops himself? He never made it past the first inquiry after he got promoted—Sams."

Roger thought about this. Up ahead, a large glowing yellow sign at the edge of the passway read WHITE ROSE in black bold letters.

"Sams was the first guy I've seen that was moved up from the row work directly. From what I'd heard, he was one of the best and got along with everyone," said Roger.

"Well I guess he won't no saint seein' as he got snipped an all."

They approached an old looking building with large dingy shutters around it. Almost completely covered by black film, the shutters were riddled with cracks.

The slider for The White Rose was an old manual one that had a hand crank to open. Once they approached the front Roger and Charly forced their way through a small crowd loitering around the entrance.

Charly reached the hand crank first and wrenched it between his short stubby fingers. He rotated the rusted metal handle in a circular motion as the slider rotated outward revealing a dimly lit, tightly packed diner with metallic blue rectangular tables with chairs attached around them.

Loud toones were booming from the back of the eatery that sounded like screeching rats. As they entered the bar, no one greeted them. Instinctively, Charly walked over to the high dark coated countertops into a crowd of people waiting to be served.

"HEYOO, two white Czechians and a table," Charly roared over the crowd hovering around the high chairs.

His short stature never matched his booming voice. Now a few of the patrons were looking at them. A slender figure with spiky blue hair and deep, sunken eyes stared at them suspiciously. Roger tried ignoring them but he felt an unyielding scrutiny.

Charly turned to the eyeing person and sized them up. "Can we help you, Hoss?"

Roger gulped, hoping that the "Hoss" title Charly had placed on the patron wouldn't offend them.

"Order a third one of those Czechians and we can talk."

Their high-pitched voice definitely had a sharp tone as if they were annoyed. In turning their seat toward Roger and Charly they noticed dark makeup and a large bulge coming from the individual's throat. Roger's hands tightened, hoping that they would at least introduce themselves so he could relax.

Charly glanced back at the barkeep as he scraped suds off two large containers oozing with white fizz. "Make it a trifecta." The barkeep looked annoyed and walked the two drinks over to them. With a grunt he slid the drinks across the countertop.

"Today's rate is 20%."

"Damn, you go higher and higher on the fees every time, Ace."

Before Charly had a chance to protest further, Roger reached into his trousers and pulled out his handheld and transferred the plinkos for the two drinks.

"We got it covered, friend, one more and we're square. Point us to the table so we can get these out of your way."

Taken aback by Roger's calm demeanor, he pointed over to one of the corners adjacent to the bar area.

"Towelettes by the mirror over there to wipe it down. I'll have Swish bring the last one over to you. Take Juss with you too—she's been getting on my nerves all day."

He looked over at the person who stared back at him with their sunken glare. She lifted her head up and staggered toward the table that had been pointed out to them.

She wore high black boots with dark black tights. Her T-shirt had a wet stain down the front. Her broad shoulders poked out the sides of her short raspberry colored shirt cut off above her belly button that showed a large metallic piercing. Charly picked up the two drinks and followed Juss over to the table.

"Who's got wiper duty?" Juss squeaked with a tone of irreverence.

Charly balked back, "I got these drinks and Rog just covered yours. So YOU grab the rag."

Juss flashed a half smile at him showing small pointed teeth and a large gap in the side of her mouth. She leaned toward a small tub near the table and grabbed the driest cloth she could find. With a few quick swipes she brushed crumbs and spilled juice off the side. By the time they sat down, Swish was walking over with the third Czechian.

"You two must be regulars here, most folk would grab their drinks to go and probably send 'em back after they hear what the current rates are."

"Yea we are used to it by now for sure," Charly returned.

Juss slid down onto a seat at the far end of the table across from where Roger and Charlie sat. She leaned over to one side as she eyed the large beverage. She was visibly intoxicated. Roger looked down at the table and noticed her right hand fidgeting as she tried to maintain upright balance.

"You sure you'll be able to handle another one…uhh, Juss?" Charly said with a snap of his finger at remembering her name. "Looks like you're already a few deep friend"

Juss tried once more to straighten her stature and forced a look over to Charly.

"Hell yea boi," she screeched as she grabbed the enormous handle of the cup, tilting it back toward her face.

"What's the occasion?" Roger asked. "Are you celebrating something or are you a regular?"

"HAA! Celebrate… What in the hell is there to celebrate in good ole Novolica? Celebrate too hard and someone may think you're up to no good. Report you faster than a hub ad. No—tonight is my night. Maybe my last—but whatever happens I ain't gone feel a thing by the morning with how much I've been throwing down. Gonna stay up all night bidin' my time."

Roger interjected, "That is a TERRIBLE idea. When you're tired you won't be able to focus as well. The X3 might flag you for mentirring cause your mind may be foggy."

Juss grimaced. Charly shifted awkwardly in his chair as a few more of Juss' teeth were now showing. The entire top row looked jaggedly cut. They fit together like puzzle pieces over the tops of the spaces against the bottom row. Her gums were excessively bright cherry red around the jigsaw puzzle fitting teeth. Though they were unnaturally white and clear- with a bright shimmer, their shape and rough looking texture drew attention away from their cleanliness.

"You can be focused all you want—that won't help anything if those Prelicans pick that day to be your last day. They change the statement, turn up the dials, or maybe they're just having a bad day. And that'll be the end of it. So better I enjoy myself now. Could be my last chance."

At that last word, Juss' large adam's apple bobbed shakily as she took another large gulp of the drink clutched in her wide hands.

"Do you know who did it?" Charly asked intently.

Juss looked over at him confused as she wiped a small droplet from her chin.

"Who reported you? Got any idea what they'll ask? From what you've already told us, it don't sound like this was planned."

Juss leaned back and folded her arms across her broad chest. Her belly button piercing made a loud clinking noise as it brushed against the table.

"Tough to say," she responded. "Been so many now, could've been anyone of 'em feeling guilty. Or jealous that I should've given 'em more attention. Then you got those who are all upset for no reason. People I've never even really met before. Always getting so worked up to see someone like me. Changing my name, moving around—it always leads to the same place. Back in those damn chairs."

"How do you manage to keep on livin' like that, eating and having a place to stay if you change your name and move? Sounds to me like you changing places all the time is what's causing all the trouble for you. All they have to do is give you a statement about who you really are."

"Wrong," said Juss matter-of-factly with a deep grunt. "Each time I change my name I do it legally through the Prelican registry. That way my career transfers over every time. If they ask me what my name is, giving them whatever it says on my statement wouldn't be mentir-ring as long as they have one of my previously registered names. I was placed in Bio Tech. There's plants in every city so I can go anywhere and pick up my career in the same field I was assigned. But it never matters because I get reported too many times."

Roger looked horrified. He could only imagine the strain someone must undergo to want to relist in the Prelican registry under a differ-ent name multiple times.

"How many times have you been called in exactly since your last registry change?" asked Roger.

Juss looked around and tightened her grip around the beverage.

"I—I've lost count. I do remember my third month as a Class 3. I was excited to take on new challenges and was looking for a way to enhance the photosynthesis process to produce twenty-five times the normal rate of oxygen in multiple plant species. I was getting close and had already started receiving recognition for the progress we had made. That's when the inquiries started coming in. The month I submitted a final analysis and test plan to enable the process—I was called in thirteen times."

"HOLY SHIT, Hoss!" Ignoring the scoffing noise from Juss at using this label, Charly continued on, "How did you get through it? Thirteen inquiries in one month would push anyone over the edge."

"Haa! I went over the edge years ago. I didn't even think I would make it this far. And you better believe I've got the scars to prove it. For God's sake I could probably create a manual on how to operate an X3 since I've seen it done so many times. And sooner or later my teeth will be so ground down I'll have to get a new set put in."

Roger let out a short grunt. He knew how it made him feel every time he'd been in that room. Strapped down tightly to that chair with one of those deadly devices anchored to your very soul. Those grueling few minutes that would determine whether you would live or die. He couldn't fathom any more than Charly experiencing this horror thirteen times in one month.

"Just hoooold on a second," Charly said in an increasingly louder voice as his beverage started to become scarce. "You said you got called in by people you don't even know. That's against the mandate. Plus if your name's getting submitted after name changes and moving, you got to be straight with yourself. What in the hell are you doing to keep pissing people off?"

Roger had been wondering the same thing. There had to be some reason why she kept getting submitted over and over. After all, most people don't take this kind of thing lightly.

Juss looked down at the table for a moment and turned the glass around a few times in her hand. She hesitated before taking a sip and saying, "I haven't done a damn thing but be myself." Anger seeped through her screechy voice.

"Why should I try to be something I'm not because who I am makes people uncomfortable? I've done nothing but dedicate my life to researching ways to help Novolica. And what do I get in return? A bunch of insecure pansies that are afraid being around me will taint their image or something. Someone like me is used to this kind of treatment. No matter where I turn or how nice I am. People take issue with who I am without even knowing me. They try to discredit my work and downplay my work ethic. Even back when I was a Class 1, my evaluators had an issue with me being interested in Biotech."

"Well at least you got your pick—" Charly interrupted.

"Anyway, I do know who it was this time. I knew what was going to happen the second he gave me that look of shame."

"The second WHO gave you a look?" Roger asked.

Juss looked more distraught now and heaved another large gulp of the drink. She let out a loud belch and slammed the glass back down onto the table.

"My uh… my boss."

She looked around the room nervously.

"He's … he's married. NOT TO ME. No, of course not. He's—well… He's been exploring himself. I've been at this location now for eight months. He's the one who gave me the position and has been mentoring me in their research department. I—I kind of suspected that he had some type of ulterior motive.

"He invited me to lunch with him two weeks ago and as we were leaving… he kissed me. Right after it happened he couldn't look me in the eye. When we got back to work he didn't leave his office for the rest of the evening. He avoided me for days. Then we made eye contact one morning when he and his wife were switching drivers for her to take their car after he'd been dropped off at work. That look… that look on his face said it all."

"Well helllll, aren't you the heartbreaker! Did ya smooch him back?" asked Charly, clearly amused about the entire situation.

Before Juss could answer, Roger interrupted. "Have you tried to confront your boss about this? Maybe talking to him would get him to drop the inquiry. This is bullshit. That prick invited you to lunch and went too far. He's the one who is married—that is on HIM to figure out. You shouldn't have to suffer due to his guilt. These halfwit assholes we have making these rules are to blame. How is that in any way fair to everyone when one person can risk another's life to save their own ass?"

Juss was startled by the support she was getting from Roger and intrigued by his passion but couldn't understand why he was so vocal about it.

"Rog, we all know that's how it is. That's what my daddy and your grandpap fought for. They wanted to Restore the nation. Forty years back. No telling how bad things might have been before."

"Or so they say. Who is really being helped when it comes to this? How many people have to get killed before someone realizes that the Prelicans don't care about anyone but their own image?"

Juss had signaled over to the bar to bring another drink out to their table.

"Either way, no one's going to be able to do anything about it before I go in tomorrow. Hopefully it's not my time. We all know it's not ideal. But maybe there are some people out there happy that this is how things are."

"Who exactly? We all know this doesn't help us and the Restoration was on shaky ground since the beginning."

"Rog, I'm surprised this is getting you all up in arms," said Charly. "Normally you aren't one to get all vocal against the Prelicans. I know it ticks you off too though."

Roger's shoulders slumped over low and his face sank. Then he had an idea.

"Hey, I know you've had your fair share of inquiries, but, my uhh— someone I know that works in engineering on mentir detection devices gave me some advice. Try ending your axion statement with PERIOD. I think it only works if you accept what they give you. But she's pretty confident that when you say this after your statement, it gives some finality to ensure the machine doesn't read you as mentirring. I know it sounds crazy, but it worked for me during my last inquiry."

Juss looked back at him perplexed. "Thanks. I wish we didn't have to go through this. The Chancellor has been in power for 40 years now and nothing will change as long as he's involved."

Roger and Charly both nodded in agreement.

"Hell, I don't know if this will ever change. He leads the Prelicans and they are loyal to him through and through. The only way we could get rid of these inquiries would be for someone else to take the Chancellor's place. After all this time, no one's even tried. Every year someone has a shot—somebody can step up and get the votes to put him out. But no one ever does. Probably never will."

"Yeah, would you sign up to get an inquiry live on the hub every month? There's a reason why he is the only person that can do that job. I bet at this point his brain isn't even physically capable of mentirring about anything. Not to mention he gets tested on the best of the best mentir machines. What are they—X5 Gold Jigs? No way in hell I'd ever sign up for that," said Juss.

"Well I guess that makes him the most trustworthy person in Novolica huh," Roger scoffed.

"We all know how things are being run and what it does to the nation. People are killed weekly and families are broken up. It's like we are powerless to stop it. Who even knows how accurate the X3's are? I am sure all of the people that get killed aren't actually mentirring. That so-called trustworthiness may be the only advantage the Chancellor has."

Once they had all finished their last round, Roger made a point to wish Juss luck during the inquiry. Charly didn't say anything about it.

After Juss left, stumbling toward the exit with her handheld outstretched in front of her to contact transportation back to her pod, Charly leaned into Roger.

"You think she'll make it through tomorra"?

"Hard to say."

"Did you see her teeth, how they had all been grinded down? She was serious about all those inquiries she's been through, no doubt about it."

"Yea she's in a tough one for sure. I mean—knowing that some spineless asshole reported her because of something he did. That is the worst inquiry to be in. There's no telling what her statement will be. I was always told to never reject the statement—that making your own is likely to get you snipped. But when the statement is a half-truth, or something like this, they could be asking her to mentir by accepting it. It's a slippery slope. One of those long walks up the hill only to find a short fast drop to the bottom—in a pool of blood."

Roger leaned back in his chair. Tired of talking about the subject, he pulled out his handheld and scrolled along the bar's food menu.

"You sure you still wanna eat? Guess we didn't see such a lively time comin' our way," Charly said.

"Yea I'm still going to grab something to go. Probably get something for Marela too, in case she's hungry."

"Well ain't that sweet," Charly replied with a grin. "So uh, when are you going to ask her to take you back?"

Roger tried to look surprised.

"Don't look at me like that, Rog. I know you been thinking it for a long time. Hell, with all that talk with Juss about inquiries coming in left and right, we can't waste any precious time these days."

Roger hesitated. "You know I can't, Charly. After what happened with Briyano... She may not ever be... you know, ready for us again. I mean I know it's been a while, but I don't want to take things too fast. Or better, I shouldn't be taking things anywhere at all."

"You got to live a little, Rog. Two years is a long time, man. Hell if you take him out of the equation, you haven't touched Marela in five years. All's I'm sayin is, if you say you're done with making any more moves on her then maybe it's time for you to move on. Get your own place away from her so you don't feel all torn up about it."

Roger took a deep breath. He would in fact be taking home two different dishes tonight. Back to the pod he shared with an ex-partner.

"Yea I figured as much," Charly snickered at him when Swish came over to their table carrying one large container with two separate orders bundled together.

CHAPTER SEVEN

Distressed Genealogy

Seeing Roger come home with two large containers and smelling the aroma of fresh baked goods sent Marela into a frenzy. She jumped to her feet, smile wide and hands clapping together rapidly.

"Oh great, I am absolutely starving," she called out.

She followed him as he crossed the room to set everything down, closely examining the labels on the top of the boxes as Roger pulled the food out.

"White Rose," she said inquisitively. "I thought you said that place was a dump."

"It is. Charly insisted we go there."

"Well it can't be all bad."

Marela eyed the food intensely as Roger slid it toward her.

"WOW, is this Chinicha? I don't believe it!"

Marela tore into the food so quickly, her spoon became a blurred line dipping swiftly back and forth between her mouth and the container.

"And it's pretty good," she said between spoonfuls of the thick, pasty looking soup. "I feel like I'm back home in La Bajo. This is making me miss it so much. Thanks, Roger. Did you know they had Chinicha there before you went?"

"Yea, I guess I noticed it one time before. Can't really remember when though."

Marela gave him a look of disbelief.

"Were there a lot of people there? Did you meet anyone new?"

"Actually yea, though it may have been better if we didn't," Roger frowned.

"What makes you say that?"

"Well...the person we met was getting twisted the night before an inquiry."

Marela's eyebrows crinkled and her body stiffened.

Maybe I shouldn't have said anything. Now I'll have to revisit this all over again.

He took a deep breath. "As soon as we walked into White Rose, we ran into a woman named Juss. She was completely wasted. She started talking to us and let us know that she had an inquiry tomorrow. Apparently because of who she is—all kinds of people try to find reasons to get her called in. This time it was her own damn boss. He Invited her out to lunch and then tried to lay one on her. Only problem is, he's married. So Juss is pretty sure his guilt is the reason for her inquiry."

"TYPICAL," Marela shouted in a loud, high voice.

"Yeah, it sucks. I mean there isn't a worse situation to be in. She said she once had thirteen inquiries in one month! Can you imagine? That is absolutely insane. The stress, the anxiety of being called in that many times. Thinking that might be the end for you again and again. That is the issue with this Restoration stuff. Why are people submitting inquiries and why would they call in one person that many times in a month? It completely goes against the trust value that is supposed to be the underlying factor. Am I wrong here?"

Marela perked up. She moved her chair closer and leaned toward him. Roger continued as her gaze deepened.

"I mean the nerve of that guy. To put someone's life in danger like that. The Chancellor says this is for the good of our nation. Maybe it's for the good of himself. Good people are suffering because of this and it's not right."

Roger's hands were balled in tight fists.

"Prelicans claim things were worse before the Restoration but they could not have been that bad. This system is terrible. We need to…" Roger hesitated.

It was as if a voice inside of him was pulling him back to Earth and letting him know he was saying too much—thinking too far outside of the box. Part of him wanted to do something, to make the system better. However, the voice prevailed and Roger thought better of it. Marela waited patiently.

"Yea… we need to… what?" she asked soothingly.

Roger shrugged. "I guess when it's all said and done, the Prelicans are running things their way—"

"You were right about everything you've said. This is not how things should be. What else were you going to say? Don't worry… you know you can tell me."

She placed a hand lightly on his knee. He felt a tingling sensation. She had not broken direct eye contact with him. This attention from Marela felt heartwarming.

"Forget it, there's nothing we can do. No sense in wasting our breath on this."

Marela pulled away from him. Her soft smile turned into a frown.

I've blown it again. I wonder if she'll just let it go.

"I know you don't really believe that, Rog. We've talked about this before and I know you see things the same way I do. That the Prelicans are full of shit and these inquiries are NOT what's best for Novolica. Sooner or later some people will step up and fight against the way things are now."

Some people… Is that directed at me? She's not going to let this go. This conversation is pointless.

Roger stood up and walked backward toward his sleeping area.

"Look, it's one thing to talk about how things should be better. But we both know that's never going to happen. That's nothing but a fantasy that will never come true."

Right? We can't change anything. How could we?

Roger took a deep breath. Ignoring Marela's disapproving looks, his eyes darted to the ceiling and the floor to avoid eye contact. Marela sat in silence, now clenching her fists.

"I CAN'T BELIEVE YOU!" she finally said in a thunderous voice. "YOU KNOW AS WELL AS I DO THAT THINGS ARE FUCKED UP HERE. AND YOU ARE CONTENT TO SIT BY AND WATCH THINGS HAPPEN TO OTHER PEOPLE. TO OUR FAMILY, FRIENDS AND DO NOTHING? I KNOW YOU'RE BETTER THAN THAT AND YOU ARE STRONGER THAN YOU THINK."

Roger shuddered and stopped in place, speechless.

"If you feel the same way I do about everything, we should do something about it. I… I know you Roger, and we've known each other for a long time. I know you could really make a difference if you wanted to."

Marela's voice had taken a considerably lower tone and she walked toward him this time as she spoke. As she neared, Roger instinctively reached his arm out toward her. In a low sweeping motion he grabbed her hand and slid his fingers through hers.

Say something… say something…

Clasping her hand, he pursed his lips tightly and softened his gaze. Marela moved closer and eyed him longingly. Her mouth hung open. Roger slipped his hand from hers and forced his smile away as he retreated to his sleeping area for the night.

～

The next day Roger told Charly about the conversation with Marela.

"That Marela is tough. She'd probably be a better Chancellor than old Prumpt himself."

Interesting take on things. I've never thought about it, but yeah that makes sense. She's always so level-headed and focuses on how to make things better.

Roger found himself running these words over and over in his mind. Even now on his way over to Cafe Por Cafe, shuffling alongside dozens of others walking along the passways zigzagging by one another. There were more people around. He had been squished to the very edge of the shiloh on the way over.

Once inside the diner, he scanned the room for the familiar face.

He spotted her at the back, wearing a bright green dress highlighting her long, graying hair. Trisha had a cup of tea in front of her. Her face lit up with a grin from ear to ear once she spotted Roger. He shuffled over to the table and slid into the chair across from her. She leaned over to hug him before pelting him with questions.

"How was it at the mines last week? Did you and Marela do anything fun together in the past few days? How is she doing by the way? Have you heard anything about Finca building those new pod developments near Honey and Fifth Street?"

Roger went through each question without elaborating much on anything. He didn't mention his and Charly's visit to the White Rose.

"You know, sometimes I wish they would lower the age to qualify as a Retro Class citizen. I'm not sure how I will manage coordinating logistics on all these development projects for another seventeen years. You would think as much time and effort you give in forty years would be enough."

"Well, I guess old grandpa should have included something in the demands of the Restoration for Novolica to lower the retro class citizen age. Seventy-eight is steep. Not to mention the inquiries."

"Everything is fashioned the way it's supposed to be. It's hard to remember him now after so many years. But daddy and I were close until he passed. His war pains had gotten so bad. I know in my heart that it was a hard-fought battle with him and the other founders to get things set up the way they are now."

Roger eyed her curiously.

"Are you sure everything is set up EXACTLY the way it is supposed to be? Your mother was killed by an inquiry."

Trisha's smile faded.

"Yes, when that happened I was devastated. At the time I could not understand why anyone would think my mother was capable of mentirring. But your father was able to get me through things and helped me see the truth about her."

"And uhh, what truth would that be?"

The corners of Trisha's mouth drooped as she continued.

"That she wasn't everything I thought she was. Daddy painted her out to be this perfect person who had everything together. But your father knew better. He was able to see her for who she truly was."

Trisha's voice was trembling. Her speech sounded slow and deliberate.

"Blynt was everything to me. He taught me everything I know and took care of me once mom was gone. I hadn't even become a career starter yet but your father made sure I found my way."

Roger gasped.

"WHAT? Are you kidding me! Ama, your relationship with Blynt started before you were twenty-one? That's against the law—there's no way this happened."

Trisha tried to calm Roger down but he was putting together the pieces. "You told me your mother's inquiry happened when you were sixteen. When did my dad start pursuing you?"

Tears swirled in her eyes. Her hands were balled tightly together.

"Your father always loved me. Since he first met me when he and my mother started living together. I think I was twelve years old then. My mother became jealous of the bond we shared and that is why she got caught for mentirring. She was always hateful and envious of me. Blynt saw right through her."

"STOP, please. I don't want to hear any more of this," Roger begged her.

His head was spinning. He felt nauseous. He tried fixing his eyes on a large hub hanging in the middle of the diner.

"Hey can you read what that says from here? It looks like there's some type of breaking news flash."

Trisha turned and squinted to read the words flashing across the large hub.

"No, it's hard to make out. Why don't we pull it over, then we can listen too."

Roger nodded shakily in agreement. They shifted the mugs on the table. Roger rubbed his hand across a small square cutout. He pressed into it, revealing a metallic keypad. He pushed a few keys, causing a small projection of the large hub in the diner to appear above their table. After reading the headline, Trisha turned a dial to increase the volume.

"MINUTES IN: Deary Mines Inc. has announced company losses and unavoidable job cuts in an effort to consolidate financial earnings. Johnson Deary, Director of Deary Mines is quoted as saying that steep reduction in labor is necessary to balance the dire financial situation. Top management is reportedly shocked and caught completely off guard, as they were under the impression the mines have been running efficiently and produced an excess of supply in GTE for the last seven quarters. Story still developing."

Trisha glanced at Roger searching for a response. His mouth lay wide open, head hanging low on his shoulders.

"I can't believe this. It has to be a mistake," he spluttered, quivering. "The mine only has a few hundred workers running everything and we've been the most productive GTE producer in Novolica! They can't get rid of anyone. That would be insane!"

Trisha scanned the small floating hub carefully. Roger crossed his arms over his stomach.

What if I'm chosen? What if I'm going to be one of the workers let go? What if I can't keep up paying my portion of the rent? Marela already makes more than me, but I would never ask her to cover me. What if she decides to move out? I'll never see her again. Oh GOD Oh GOD.

Trisha grabbed his wrist and said, "ROG, it's O-K. Breathe for a second."

Roger looked at her. His eyes had gone glassy.

"How can I breathe, Ama? I could lose my career today?"

"Lose it or not, you'll always have a means to live, Rog. Whatever happens, the outcome is out of your hands. No use in getting all worked up about it. The system is made to help with things like this. You resubmit your name and they'll have you placed somewhere else in less than six weeks."

"But WHY? This isn't supposed to happen, right?" He looked at her imploringly.

"In Novolica, we are assigned where we stay our entire careers. We shouldn't have to go through the placement process all over again. I was picked to start at the La Finca mine rows when I was twenty-one. Like everyone else! This is where I'm supposed to be—and not to mention—"

"Yes, you scored so high on all of the aptitude tests. I remember your career starter ceremony. Awww, you were so nervous Rog—and when they finally assigned you, I thought you were going to faint." A wide grin spread across her face as she closed her eyes, reminiscing.

"Well, that's part of the issue. I'm barely a career settler. And come to think of it, there aren't many workers down at the rows who are even close to retro class. If we are all still so young, how do they expect us to find somewhere else? We got assigned! The assignments are supposed to guarantee us job security, right?!" Roger's voice boomed as his words echoed loudly.

Trisha shook her head. "Well, it doesn't work that way. People move around, sometimes even change their selected career altogether. I've seen it happen. Only a few times in all my years but I know it's possible."

"All of those aptitude tests and personality evaluations. It was constant badgering and figuring out where you were going to be placed. It was miserable. The only thing I liked about being Class 1 was that we didn't get mentir screening. And now I see. It was all just… SUCH A WASTE OF TIME! Why would they make kids go through all these tests knowing that one day it may change? All of that to get pushed out before even reaching ten years in."

"Roger, calm down."

"No, the mine rows have been operating at top capacity for months now. There is no way the company is losing money. There must be enough GTE stored to power the city for years. I met with Johnson Deary. He told me how great the company was doing. As an executive, he would definitely know the truth. Although right before he kicked me out of his office, there had been someone on the phone with him. It was someone who had been pressuring him into doing something he didn't want to do."

"Rog, I am sure you will be fine. I know you work hard. They would never fire you," Trisha assured him.

She pulled out a much wider handheld from her bag sitting under the table.

"You'd better get down there, it's almost time for your shift to start."

A large lump in Roger's throat made him unable to swallow. He tucked his handheld that was sitting out on the table into his slit pocket and stood up slowly.

"I will call you and let you know how things go today. I'm sure you're right that everything will be fine."

After letting out a deep sigh, he made for the exit. Roger looked back at his mother once more and with one last wave of his hand, he passed through the slider. Outside, everything he walked past turned to a blur.

CHAPTER EIGHT

Resource Action

Roger approached the mine, nearing the large metallic structures bulging from the ground. *What's going to happen to everyone? Charlie, Sunny, all the other employees?*

There was commotion all around. Surrounding the field area leading to the GTE towers and in the passways in front of the facility were crowds of hub reporters and onlookers. Large passenger transports with hub stations logos imprinted on them were visible in the lot and workers scattered about near them. People trotting around with large audio grabbers in hand, followed by others with brightly colored handheld devices held close to their faces.

I can't believe the hub stations are here. People are actually interviewing with them.

Roger kept his head down and forced through the crowd to the entrance. He felt someone grab his arm as multiple people moved in front of him with audio grabbers.

"What do you think has happened at the most productive mine row in Novolica to cause this abrupt and devastating announcement?" the hub reporter asked him.

Another reporter crowded in. "What is it like working at the mine rows every day? Would you say the job is enjoyable?"

"Is the leadership in place to blame for the misfortunes falling on the career settlers here?" demanded yet another reporter.

Jeez I wonder what other people are answering.

"Uhh, no comment."

Trying to force his way through, he knocked an audio grabber out of one of the tech's hands.

"Sorry about that," he said quickly as he turned toward the man who was now picking up the device.

Scowling, he examined the round transparent dish in his hands. His expression lightened and he carefully pointed it back toward the hub rep standing adjacent to him with a handheld close to his mouth. He was yelling loudly trying to get anyone to stop and talk with him. Roger pressed on toward the entrance, where he was met by two security guards standing on opposite sides of the slider.

There's never been security posted here before. This is bad.

He reached for his handheld and held it up to the scanner to confirm his ID. A large photo of him appeared on the display as the word CONFIRMED blinked rapidly in green. Roger proceeded through.

"HOLD UP—YOU AREN'T GETTING IN," one of the security guards spoke in a deep, edgy sounding voice.

A beefy arm brushed past Roger's shoulder as he turned around. The two security guards were barring a hub rep trying to enter the courtyard behind Roger. The small skinny man was now being lifted off the ground by his arms, tightly gripped by the two security guards. One of them looked sideways at Roger and smiled.

"Don't ya worry, we've been paid to make sure this lot doesn't get in and bother you and the row workers. Go ahead and we'll make sure this weasel can't follow you."

Just glad it's not me being hoisted up.

The commotion continued inside the courtyard. Angry faces were all over. Mine row workers, managers, and directors were shouting and debating loudly.

Just go to work. Focus. We'll be ok. Nothing to do but work until something happens.

Roger reached his personal storage compartment and retrieved the finger sheaths.

"WHAT THE HELL! I NEED THIS, MAN.".

"NO WAY I'M LEAVING THIS PLACE."

"THEY'RE AXING US FOLKS, THEY DON'T GIVE A SHIT!"

Roger slid on the finger sheaths, trying to ignore all of the yelling and commotion. Then he heard a familiar voice behind him.

"NOW RELAX, THIS IS GONNA GET FIGURED OUT! OUR GUYS WON'T LEAVE US OUT TO DRY."

Roger searched through the ruckus for his friend with his back-wood, burly tone voice booming over others. He forced his way through the large mob gathering as a short, hard hand grabbed his shoulder forcefully.

"Rog! Wheeew, I've never seen the rows like this. What were they thinking announcing something like that on the national hub? They had to expect people to react like this. No way to avoid it."

Charly seems so calm with everything that's going on. I'm glad to see him at least.

"You aren't worried at all about what will happen?"

"No sir, I know they're not lettin' me go. And hey even if they did, I been a Class 3 for eight years. My evaluation could've gone a bunch of ways. Now I got proof I can do a job."

"So what do we do? Do we start working, do we wait for someone to tell us who's out?"

People began rushing over to the center of the atrium. Roger and Charly followed the crowd. The directors were grouped together on a raised platform in front of everyone.

"THERE HE IS! If there is anyone that can pull this together for us it's Sunny," someone yelled.

Sunny was standing in front of the other directors, fidgeting with a voice multiplier. He bobbled it up closer to his face and made a few selections on the display. He wasn't wearing his signature metallic tie, though the rest of his clothing was perfectly pressed as usual.

He cleared his throat loudly and it echoed throughout the court-yard. All the commotion and chatter quieted. Roger squinted up toward the elevated platform.

Sunny looks nervous. He's sweating and I can see his hands shaking from here.

"Guys, ve awe going to be OK."

He paused for a moment, fighting hard to maintain his composure.

"Ve awe howad de HUB. Ve know dis is awe of a sudden and NO—dis is NOT yow fault. Evewy wokah in dis mine row has been mowa than suitable at opewations. Awe leadawshup team made a decision that vwill now affect all of us. Vwe work togeder like bwovas. Dis announcement vwill not destroy us. Yes—some of you vwill no longoh be here evewey day. It will be challenging for dose leaving and dose dat will be coming back tomowoh."

Voices murmured throughout the audience.

"Yes," he responded. "Today will be an off day fowa eveweyone. Af-toh ve have made dis announcement and send yowa caweewa status to your handheld, you awe fawee to go!", "Ve do not take any pawide in dis and a LOT of caweful considawation, vwe have identified 350 individuals vwe need to provide a package fowa vwit owa appaweciation fowa evewey day and evewey thing you awe have done fowah us here at Deary Mines Inc."

People started shuffling about as if the entire crowd was turning circles in place. This was going to be very hard to swallow. Roger looked over at Charly. His smile had transformed into a snarl.

Wow, now even Charly is at a loss for words. I'm all out too. There was hushed chatter amongst the crowd.

Sunny went on, "I vwill be puwasonally vwoking wit de oda main caweeya locations hewa in Finca. I believe vwe will be able to find new jobs fowa evewey single wowka we awe being fowaced to let go. You awe all talented and have led us to some of ouwa best yewas hewa at dis mine row. Three-hundred-fifty of our wokas is ova thirty powacent.

Dis numba is not small and I can tell you dis was one of de hawdest dings I have had to do in my life."

Some people started to sit down in place. Others put their heads into their hands. The ones who were recording had put away their handhelds. Despite his visible distress, Sunny's respect from everyone present was unquestionable.

He forced one final smile as big as he could muster as his eyes filled with liquid. He slowly turned and walked off of the platform as the tears began to flow. His exit was immediately met with applause. There were chants of support for him. The clapping dragged on longer than intended.

Once things had finally died down, another director stepped onto the platform. Jason Stinner was not as well-liked as Sunny. In fact, most of the mine row workers despised him for his harsh leadership style.

Charly once caught him sleeping up in the director tower during the workday when he had to go up and get approval to change a few of the settings on the generators to dial back the pump process. When he woke up and realized that Charly saw him, he ticketed him for insubordination on account of his questioning of the dial settings.

"Now that we have all the logistics out of the way," Stinner said, "we'll need to talk about our strategy going forward. Since we'll be down a few bodies, we'll be on extended hours to make sure the production won't slow down. All shifts will be from 06:30 to 19:00 hours. Breaks will be cut and allocated on a weekly basis. Lastly, mid-day lunch will be adjusted from 11:00 to 12:00. We'll be enforcing the new plan rigorously.

"If you happen to receive the 'Do Not Return' message, be sure to clear out your storage compartment today—any leftover contents will be put in the incinerators first thing tomorrow morning. We are also turning off building access today so you will not be able to reenter without an escort. Any questions?"

The mood of the crowd had shifted and a beastly ferocity was now filling the space. There were people shouting and others raising their fists in the air toward the platform. Stinner's every word felt like licks of venom. He didn't seem to care at all. Everyone was now standing again. Sobs had been replaced with battle cries. Stinner fumbled through the settings on the voice device. With a quick swipe of his index finger, his voice was magnified even more as he attempted to preside over the crowd again.

"I know, I know what you are all thinking," he tried to say with conviction. "This isn't what we wanted. None of us—I assure you. But this is coming from higher than all of us. Shit rolls downhill and we are waiting at the creek for it to push us right in.

"I wish I had better news but that's what we have to work with. The messaging is set to go out in one hour. Once you get your status, we would like everyone to act accordingly. The warehouse and courtyard are both shutting down at 13:00 hours. If anyone has any concerns, be sure to submit your question on your handheld. We will stay strong," Stinner concluded and then casually leaped out of sight from the platform.

People surged toward the platform abruptly in an attempt to try and hold Stinner for more questions. It was too late. He had already retreated back into one of the director's break areas. People pushed and shoved. Most were still yelling, some sobbing quietly. Others had given up and were heading for the exit. Roger looked at Charly. His fists were balled up and his bulking muscles fully flexed.

"Well hell," Charly finally spoke out. "That son of bitch has given us an hour to wait and see if we're never coming back here again. Who the hell thought it was a good idea to keep us waiting like this to see if we're going to be switching careers? They absolutely need to be fired for that stupid shit."

"OI, CHARLY!"

A voice beckoned from a short distance away. It was Dexter Hughes, one of the oldest employees still working the rows. Dexter was heavy-set with a thick brown puffy beard. One of the few rules of a mine row employee's appearance was no long hair to avoid getting pulled downward into any of the sprockets while they were pumping—therefore Dexter kept his beard well trimmed, giving his face the look of an overweight furry kitten.

He wobbled toward the two of them in a hurried fashion, with anger practically steaming from his ears.

"Who... the... hell... does Johnson Deary think he is pulling something like this?! I know it...I knowww that this came from him directly! Only someone at his level can make a call like this."

At hearing this, Roger thought back to his meeting with Johnson Deary. He didn't think he had the personality to make a call like this at all.

"Have you met Deary before?" Roger asked.

"Well... yea I did, one time, in passing."

I wonder how much Dexter got to know just by passing him.

"To me he didn't seem like someone who would do something like this."

Charly chimed in, "Yea, you are right Rog. I've heard people talk about him that have had words. He's a straight shooter, no nonsense. I bet this was Stinner's strategy. Dex, you think you're safe since you've been here so long?"

Dexter took a deep breath and rested his fists on his hips.

"Hell, I don't think ... no, I may not make it. They've been... ahhemm... trying to get rid of me for years."

He took another big inhale of air.

"Thinking my beard is too close to the limit...and I'm not fit to work, and the like. I'm expecting to get that message today. I'm going...ahurrr... over to get my stuff out of my compartment."

"So what will you do next if you do get the bad message?" asked Roger.

Though he was asking Dexter, he somehow felt like he may need to know for himself. Dexter turned to face Roger.

"Don't even...don't ask me that, Rog. You are one of the ones I know that will definitely be coming back tomorrow. As ughhh for me…I'm switching over to building if that back-up option Sunny was talking about doesn't pan out. Pods and the like. My test back… in the day… I could've done either."

Hearing this, Charly looked full on angry now.

"After so much time here—Dex, you're pushing sixty, bud! Only another eighteen and you'll be eligible for retro class. You shouldn't have to switch now."

"Hell…ahaha… old change of scene may be nice to me," responded Dexter.

After these words, Dexter waddled away to the personal compartment area. Roger turned back to Charly. "I'm going to clean out my stuff and go back to the pod." Before Charly could reply, Roger quickly interjected.

"Just in case man, don't wanna lose anything. Will you be sticking around until the message comes out?"

"Damn right, if I get cut, someone around here will damn well hear about it. I understand what ya got to do. I will give you a buzz tonight."

The two turned in opposite directions, both feeling a whirlwind of emotions and tingling with uncertainty.

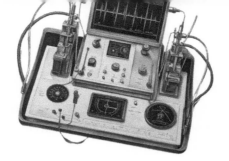

CHAPTER NINE

Mockery from A Menace

Returning to the mine after the painful layoff of thirty percent of their employees was devastating. Hardly anyone said a word to one another. No one gathered.

"Makes no damn sense for the company to be doing this good and then go and cut that many people. They got Dexter, they got Jim Soto. Hell, even Lister man. He came out with us to the White Rose a while back," said Charly.

"It just feels different around here," replied Roger. "People have this look of defeat. Everyone is just kind of going through the motions."

"I heard Steve Dobs, you know the lead engineer under Stinner, say Deary has been on fire. I'll be damned if he has something to be upset about. Word is there was some federal funding cut. Deary couldn't do anything about it. At least he still has a job though."

Roger shook his head disapprovingly.

That evening, he arrived home much later than usual due to the extended workday. Mindlessly, he turned on the hub, only leaving his trance-like state when Marela arrived.

"Hey Rog, how'd it go today after everything?"

"Not good. Everyone's in a mood. It's still hard to believe all this has happened—it was so abrupt."

"Yea, companies almost never have to get rid of career workers and definitely not on the scale that they are doing it at the mine. Did you find out anything more on why they had to do it at all?"

"Well not exactly, only a bunch of rumors. Something about federal funding being cut could be the reason why."

"WAIT!" Roger yelled loudly as he jumped up off the couch.

"That day I was in his office, Johnson Deary took a call from someone who was threatening him."

"You were in the executive's office? WOW—you didn't tell me that," Marela said teasingly.

"Yea, one day he invited me up for elixir and we chatted. He really seemed genuine. Everything was going well until he got a call from someone. Someone he called Mr. Minler or Mr. Marineford or something. I can't exactly remember—but I do remember his expression. One minute he was happy and sharing with me all the GTE we've been producing for Novolica. The next minute he looked absolutely distraught on this call right before he sent me away. This must have been what he was asking him to do on that call. That was only two weeks ago."

Marela followed him closely as he paced back and forth past the hub running the daily news feed.

"Who would have the power to force an executive to cut that many people from their workforce? Rog, LOOK—the story is on the hub again."

Marela pointed to the words flowing across the screen in red letters:
CHANCELLOR ADDRESSES FINCA MINE ROW LAYOFFS

Roger returned to his place on the couch and turned up the volume. Chancellor Prumpt was approaching a small platform with audio grabbers facing toward him. He looked as staunch as ever with stiff hair and pale skin. He was looking at the hub reps surrounding the platform he was standing on and gestured to one of them to ask their question.

"Chancellor, should other career workers be worried that one of the largest employers in Finca abruptly let go of over thirty percent of their labor force?"

The Chancellor answered with a twisted grin.

"Not at all. I have no clue what those idiots down at Deary Mines are doing. I'll tell you what, if I was running that company they wouldn't be losing plinkos all over the place. That company would be so profitable, I would be adding hundreds of career starters each year. When something like this takes place, you have to look at the leadership. I can tell you that the leadership at Deary Mines is incredibly incompetent. They don't know what the hell they are doing."

Another hub reporter threw their handheld in the air. In similar fashion the Chancellor gestured toward them with a head nod.

"Chancellor, a lot of videos have circulated in support for the people working at that mine row. These videos have garnered a lot of attention for the employees as well as the director that was heartbroken by the news of laying off so many people. Can you comment on this?"

The Chancellor laughed loudly.

"There's nothing to say there. A bunch of off the rocker second level managers probably have something to do with their problems. Did you see that guy giving the speech? You couldn't understand a damn thing he was saying. Seeing him shake all over the place while trying to give that shitshow of an address was absolutely pitiful."

The Chancellor made a fake shaking motion with his arm moved up in front of his chest. "'WE WE WE GOTTA STIIIIIICK TOGEEDER!' How in the hell did that guy ever get that job? I mean come on. Looks like they got him right out of a mental institution."

At this, a few of the hub reps awkwardly shuffled in place, unsure of how to respond. The Prelicans standing around Chancellor Prumpt applauded loudly and cackled fiercely at these remarks. The audience was absolutely speechless. It was as though some invisible hand had yanked from them every single question or comment they had prepared for the event. All of the non Prelicans stood deathly still. Roger and Marela both followed suit and stared at the hub. The Chancellor continued at the egging on of his followers:

"DiS DuHH hAwdEsT Deeng In mY LIfE!" He made fake sobbing noises. "That jag-off should've been on the list himself. Next time Deary, why don't you spare him the discomfort—as best you can that is—and let him go too. Long live our nation restored!"

He ended with a swift wave to the crowd and moved out of sight. Marela pulled out her handheld and searched frantically as she stared intensely at the small display. Roger had to force himself to look away from the hub. His fists were clenched so tight, his arms were trembling. His breath became raspy, each exhale filling his cheeks. Marela found what she was looking for. With the flick of her finger, she sent a video from her handheld to the hub. Roger's gaze hardened as he watched with her.

"It's Sunny!"

The hub channel was playing Sunny's address over again. Roger jumped to his feet, fists still tightened. The veins in his arms and neck bulged as his entire body tensed. Marela sat expressionless. Tears began rolling down her cheeks.

"So this is why you always say everyone at the mine loves Sunny."

Roger turned away from the hub and began pacing hard from one end of the room to the next. Marela turned off the console and walked over to block his path. Though Roger tried to avoid it, she met his gaze and stared longingly into his eyes, waiting for him to say something.

"That asshole. How…how dare he. How could any human being, I mean."

Marela paused for a moment, trying to find the right words to calm him down.

"I see what you mean now. I can tell Sunny is special and really cares about everyone that works for him."

Roger nodded, still trying to avoid her large brown eyes.

"I could spit out lava right now. I won't stand for this. There is no way in hell people are letting this go. Prumpt can't say whatever he wants without consequences."

"You're right," Marela agreed, "he absolutely shouldn't be able to. But he DOES. This isn't the first time he's insulted and belittled people. He's known for saying stuff like this all the time. The only way to stop this is for someone to stand up to him. Don't you think?"

Roger leaned his ear in closer to her.

"Novolica should have never been led by this guy."

Roger stood still.

"I wonder what everyone else at the mines thinks about this. Sunny...we love Sunny. Prumpt won't get away with this."

Marela slowly reached for his arm and unclenched his fist. Their eyes met. She grabbed his free arm and placed it around her waist. She moved in closer to him. They were now centimeters apart.

"We're going to do something about this. I can help you. It's not right. We deserve better. And your friend deserves better too," she whispered.

Her words danced softly around him.

I - I can't resist it anymore. She's so perfect.

Roger pulled Marela in even closer and embraced her. She let go of his hand and wrapped both her arms around his neck, holding onto him as tightly as she could. They caressed one another.

She said she wants us to take action together. That's all she wants. Another Briyano to start a revolution together. She doesn't really care about me.

Roger slowly released her. He forced himself to back away.

"I'm going to get some rest,", he said wearily.

He turned and headed toward his room. She showed the faintest smile as he moved away from her.

～

Anger was festering throughout the mine row once Roger arrived the next day. Everyone had now seen the Chancellor's hub release about their renowned leader. Sunny, never one to shy away from a challenge, was taking this head on.

He tried encouraging people to let it go and that it wasn't a big deal.

His bright shiny Restoration tie had found its way back around his neck. However it only made people more upset that he was not at all hurt by the comments made. Sunny was a strong supporter of the Chancellor and everyone knew it.

"I'm damn serious," said Charly to a group of fellow employees that had found a storage area out in the fields away from any eavesdropping.

"We could get rid of that son of a bitch. You know the Nation Renewal is only a few weeks away. There are hundreds of thousands of people all around Novolica that want to see his ass outta there. Hell, we got seven hundred here that would tie in with any damn body other than Prumpt. All they would need is twenty percent. It's right there in the damn Restoration Mandate."

Charly pulled out his handheld and shook it in the air furiously.

"Who's gunna do it?!"

The determination in his voice was unwavering. He was as furious as everyone else there, though no one would dare stand up and run outright against the Chancellor.

"How bout you, Rog?" Charly shot him a straight look to where he was sitting at the edge of the group.

Roger was listening intently but had been facing the other way, watching for anyone that might come wandering by.

"You can't be ser—"

"I'M DAMN SERIOUS!"

Charly speaking in this heightened tone stung.

"If you're so serious, why aren't you volunteering to go up against the Chancellor? You could submit your name, birth date, pod location, family relationships, EVERYTHING tomorrow and you would be perfectly eligible to go up against him. But you're not, because you know like every one of us that going against the Chancellor is a death wish.

"No one challenges the Prelicans and no one volunteers to get more inquiries. Going public like that would put a big target on your back. Guaranteed you would get four inquiries before the recall ever happens. And for what—for Prumpt to win again and humiliate you, if you make it that far? What can we do here in the mine rows but take care of each other and try to save ourselves from more risk of being called in? That's how we survive. Ignore him, and deal with what we've been given."

Roger took a few deep breaths. Everyone was looking at him in awe.

"Wow, I knew you had it in you Rog... looks like you're trying to convince yourself more than us," Charly sneered.

"It's time," a voice called out to the group.

Everyone picked up their gear and dispersed to various stations on the rows. Charly and Roger headed in the same direction. As they walked back to their posts, a few of the other workers patted him on the back and looked at him reassuringly.

I'll be ok. No one will submit my name with how angry everyone is about Sunny. Something just doesn't feel right about this. We can't just let Sunny be ridiculed that way. I'm glad I said something. Anything.

Roger walked staunchly, reliving the moment over and over.

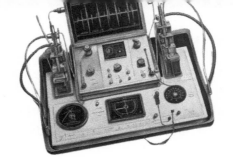

CHAPTER TEN

Life of Pain

Two weeks after the employee layoff at the mine, Roger and Marela were sitting in their pod when Roger received a floating message on his handheld.

Roger- have to reschedule our meetup tomorrow, called into inquiry in the morning

Roger read this over and over again. Each time slower, more deliberately. His expression sank as his eyes widened. His breathing became hard to manage.

"What's wrong Rog. What does it say?"

Marela noticed the look of deep concern on his face.

He tried calling her. No answer. He dialed it over and over, to no avail. He pulled the handheld away from his face and opened the message again.

"It's… it's Trisha. She uhh—got called in for an inquiry tomorrow morning."

Marela gasped loudly and threw her hands over her mouth.

"Who would dare?!! WHY?!!"

"No idea."

She's been called in. My mother. What will happen to her? There's so much I need to say. So much I need to tell her. I need to see her, to talk to her again. No, it will be ok. Nothing will happen. She'll go in, be screened and come out. We'll be meeting again next week. I'll go there. I'll go to her right now, I don't care how far it is. But will that only make her screening more difficult?

Roger tried taking deep breaths. Yet the room seemed to be without oxygen. A warm embrace encircled his neck and shoulders. Marela was hugging him tightly. He could breathe now. They didn't speak. Nothing needed to be said. They only felt. As the hub continued to buzz with noise and background programs showing, they wistfully fell asleep in each other's arms.

Marela's long curly hair had been pulled to one side exposing her soft smooth skin,. Roger's face now rested on her chest. She held onto his arm as they wrapped together, tightly wound. When Roger awoke the next morning, her warm body was gone and had been replaced with a thick covering. He reached for his handheld to check the time, 06:08. It was still early. He listened for any noise coming from Marela's bedroom. Complete silence. He slid the cover off and walked toward his pod for a morning wash.

I need to clear my mind. Ama, she's going to be called in any minute. She'll be there, strapped to the chair. Moments to decide whether she lives... or... or.

He pushed himself through his routine and headed to work.

When Roger arrived at the mine rows, he hadn't eaten anything. He was almost late and rushed in to start. He dawdled about, waiting for Trisha's "all clear" auto message but it hadn't arrived yet.

It will be ok. It will be ok, she'll message any minute now.

Halfway through the day, his handheld rang loudly during lunch hour. Roger stared at it. After an endless time loop, he answered it. He scooted away from his coworkers and listened intently, waiting for the news. In an instant, he dropped his handheld. It toppled to the floor, along with Roger.

On his knees, Roger began wailing in agony. The pain was too much. His body convulsed. Charly ran over to him and put his hand on his shoulder. The noise was piercing and the other workers around had fallen completely silent.

No one had ever seen Roger this way. Charly tried to comfort him as others moved closer. No one said anything, yet stood by his side. After an eternity, Roger forced deep breaths through his lungs in an effort to control himself. He tried to hoist himself up, but he couldn't do it. His legs felt like spaghetti noodles. Charly tried to assist in lifting him up. Roger's large frame against Charly's short body wasn't budging. Soon the other employees moved toward them. Roger was pulled to his feet by eight other mine row workers and guided to his belongings that had been neatly placed for him.

"My, my handheld," Roger said shakily as he felt his empty pockets. He looked back toward the spot he had dropped it. As soon as he turned, someone brandished a clear device that was showing static on the screen. Roger looked up at him and gave a nod of appreciation.

He tapped the display a few times to get the static to disappear. After a few shakes, the screen was clear again and a location dot beeped silently in front of him. He tucked the handheld into his pocket and hoisted a small pack over his shoulder. Roger moved toward the courtyard sluggishly, still lightly weeping.

"Rog, I can go with ya, no need for you to do this on your own. I'll talk to Sunny—I know he wouldn't—"

Charly stopped abruptly as Roger waved him off weakly. Everyone throughout all of the mine rows knew when he passed them. They gave him gestures showing their support. A few people walked over to him and gently touched his shoulder. He received two more embraces, one of which came from someone whose eyes were as wet as his.

They know. They've all been through this too. There's not a single person in Novolica that hasn't felt this same pain. Why should I be any different?

Roger arrived at the main slider, everyone else now out of sight. He took one last deep breath and wiped the tears obscuring his vision. Through the slider he went.

This has to stop. No one should have to endure this pain. Something has to be done.

～

Trisha's memorial was held in Leiton City where she had lived most of her life and Roger had grown up. Like all other citizens who had been found guilty of mentirring, her body was disposed of immediately after her next of kin confirmed her identity.

The memorial had a hololight shown of her in remembrance. There would be no ceremonial float into the ocean nor would they be able to coat her body in traditional oil. Trisha's remaining family members were there, all five of whom stemmed from Roger's half-sister Susan, who had been born before his parents got married. Susan explained to her four children her relation to her stepmother.

Marela showed up alongside her younger sister Angela, Charly with a few dozen mine row workers alongside him, Sunny, and a man who claimed he worked with Trisha for many years. They mourned. As her memories were displayed, Marela comforted Roger. After the ceremony, Roger decided to stay in Leiton City to feel the connection to his childhood and his mother.

A few nights later, Roger found himself crumpled on the floor of an inn.

"Why, WHY did this happen?" he yelled loudly.

No one answered him.

"Why does this happen over and over again to everyone in this godforsaken country? Every inquiry I've ever had. Every person I know that has been hooked up to those machines. Every single time. There's a chance, there's a chance we don't come out."

The hub was playing loudly through the evening news.

NEW MINERAL DEPOSITS DISCOVERED AT THE HEART OF NOVOLICA

Roger wept as he tried clearing his throat.

All for some leader that openly mocks good citizens—good people who love doing their jobs and helping others.

CLASS 1 CITIZENS TEST ENHANCED FOR MORE ACCURATE CAREER PLACEMENT

Roger's face turned hard. He exhaled forcefully, clasping his elbows tightly.

No more, I'm not taking it anymore. Nor should anyone else. I'll deliver everyone to something better. No one should ever have to feel this way again.

RENEWAL PERIOD NOW THROUGH THE END OF THE MONTH FOR CHANCELLOR PROSPECTS

He jerked his head up, looking at the hub announcement.

Now's the time when we can submit ourselves to challenge the Chancellor. I'll have to be screened. NO—I've passed inquiries before. I'm not afraid. I refuse to be. My mother wasn't afraid.

He looked down at his handheld, searching for the Novolica official website. There it was on the front page. The application to submit himself as a Prospect.

Something has to change. If I don't do it, no one will. For Ama. I'll get rid of these screenings for good.

Roger began filling it out. Line-by-line, detail by-detail. Inputting who he was into the application. It required him to specify his full name, date of birth, current residence, career, date of last screening, next of kin, and so on. He listed Charly, Marela, and Sunny as references. When he finished, his palms were sweaty, his head throbbing, and his legs were trembling under him.

There's no turning back once this is in. It will be public. I'll be public. No, this is insane. I can't do this.

He put the handheld down beside him. His fingers stiffened. His eyes were closed, head bowed over. Roger's heart could be heard pounding loudly through his chest. Large droplets of sweat rolled down his face.

He forced his eyes open again. Picking up the device and now staring directly at the last screen. The final submission button highlighted. His eyebrows twitched.

This is for my mother. If I don't do this, other people will feel this same pain. No one should ever feel this again.

With one finger, he moved closer and closer to the highlighted button.

I know, I know what I'm doing. There's no turning back now.

He moved his finger closer, bent and steady.

He smashed the tip of his index into the button.

It was done. Roger Aimes was on the ballot.

CHAPTER ELEVEN

Build The Base

"We have to start setting up appearances now. People need to know who you are and that you are going to be opposing the Chancellor."

Marela was beaming at Roger.

How is she so calm about this? And she already has a plan to help.

"I have a friend that lives in La Bajo with a career in public communications. She works for a network that can upload to the hub."

"Great, so are you going to call her to meet us here?"

"No, it's better we go to La Bajo. That way she will have everything she needs to introduce you. Also, there are a lot of people in La Bajo that want the Chancellor gone for good."

"Well, I'm convinced."

"How much time do we have until the public announcement?"

Roger pulled out his handheld and read the detailed message he had received once he submitted his name as a candidate.

"Looks like the public announcement is in two weeks. The process could last up to six months after the first public event, and if I get enough support—if I receive at least twenty percent of the citizens' support—I will be granted approval to move forward with an official election. In which case public debates will be scheduled at a later date."

"In that case we have to go now! We can't waste any time."

"Well, I had planned on going back to the mine rows this week since I have been out for a few days."

"Beating the Chancellor is going to be a full-time commitment, Roger. When you go in this week, you are going to have to tell them what you are doing. That way they can give you time off to start campaigning. In that case, we'll need to hold off on the La Bajo trip until after the public announcement."

"Ok, I'll let them know. Then I'll ask for another leave of absence. I wonder how they'll take the news."

Roger and Marela strategized for hours. Marela spoke with passion and resolve that ignited the two of them. They were determined to see this through.

The next day, Roger approached the leaders at the mine row to inform them of his plan. To his surprise, Sunny and the other leaders already knew he submitted himself to challenge the Chancellor. He found himself back in the Deary conference room up on the top floor again at the end of the workday. Present were Sunny, Johnson Deary, Jason Stinner, Alexa Costa the Chief of Operations, and Jill Shipman the Business Chair and Executive Function Overseer.

"I say let him do it," started Deary. "Part of the process of Mr. Aimes submitting himself is for us to be notified. It's only a formality. Give him the time he needs to prepare."

"We've just lost a large portion of the workforce, now is not a good time to allow people weeks of leave at a time. Besides, there's no way he stands a chance in the renewal process," said Stinner.

Roger shifted nervously in his chair.

It seems like they'll never come to a consensus.

"Let's say he does stand a chance," said Jill hesitantly. "We would have a lot to gain by having one of our own in that position."

"Preposterous. Our administration has gotten this company and this nation where it is today. Favorable conditions for all. I won't allow someone to try and change that. I say he works and we force an end to this escapade."

Alexa sounded sharp in her tone. Jill clutched her wrist tightly as Deary scoffed loudly at hearing this.

"Yes, I am in agreement," said Stinner smiling.

They exchanged looks of approval with one another.

"Now wait just a second, he is already registered. There's nothing any of us can do about that. In fact, actively working to hinder that process could very well be against the law," Deary pointed out.

"Precisely," agreed Jill.

Alexa looked down at her notes. "What kind of legal implications are we expecting from dictating the work schedule of our own employee?"

"I can assure you, it is not the type of legal attention this company needs right now. Regardless of the outcome, the publicity would be detrimental to investors," responded Jill.

"Some of those investors include members of the cabinet," added Stinner.

"Those cabinet members will no longer dictate how we run our business, dropping this mess on us," responded Deary fiercely.

"Those cabinet members are helping the nation run efficiently, watch your tone," Alexa snapped.

Jill's hands tightened on her hover chair armrest. Roger clasped his hands together, barely breathing. Sunny looked shaky but leaned over to Roger and placed a hand on his shoulder.

"I vwas suhpawised to see dis noteefication about you, VRoger. Vwe vwant to suppawt you howevoh vwe can in dis difficult situation. Even doh many of us suhppawt de Chancellor, you have de right to vwork towohd vwhat you believe." Sunny stood up.

"Vreegawedless of how vwe awe feel, VRoger desowves a chance to be de leadoh he believes in. It is owbveeous he needs at least one month to fully prepayoh himself. VRoger is an exceelant conchwibutah, and vwe hab planty of people det vwould be vwilling to covah his vwole down dayoh."

The room was quiet. Sunny sat down, resolved.

"Thank you Sunny, let's make it two months. As he said, there are people willing to pick up Roger's work while he's out and we owe him a fair chance," Deary said.

This time, everyone agreed. There was not a single detractor. They took a vote to solidify the decision. Once they had finished, everyone left the room except for Deary.

"I'm glad we sorted that all out," he said looking at Roger.

"We need you to win this thing. What else do you need to make it happen? I have a few contacts around Novolica that could help you with what to say. Richard Valiant, Maria Fuerte, Jennifer Greatsong. Have you heard any of these names? They are all wealthy business leaders, friends of mine. They each have their own special skills and I can connect you with them. These are people who want to see you successful in this endeavor. I'm sure you'll need to get around quickly from city to city, otherwise you'll be at a disadvantage."

Deary paused for a moment and then looked seriously at Roger.

"I'm willing to let you use my personal power glider if you need to get somewhere fast. Though you'll need to tell me a few weeks in advance in case I need to adjust my schedule. And don't worry about the time off. If you need more, I'll make sure you get an extension on your leave of absence."

"I really appreciate everything, Mr. Deary. I'll finish today and then take the time off to prepare."

The two shook hands and Deary ushered him back to the lower levels.

Charly was happy to help spread the message as far and loud as he could. He circled around the entire facility, determined to let everyone know that Roger was going to take the Chancellor's place. The employees at the mine remembered what The Chancellor had said about Sunny on the hub which led to many supporting Roger. Only a handful were against his candidacy and shied away from pledging their support. By the end of the workday, Roger had received more pats on the back, hugs, and handshakes than he had in his entire eight year tenure at the mine.

Charly walked with him to the shiloh station. He never looked prouder as he stared back at Roger. They soon parted ways and with all of the energy he could muster Charly shouted, "WE ARE GONNA HAVE A NEW CHANCELLOR IN TOWN!"

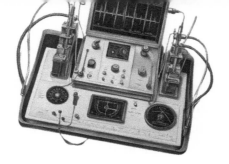

CHAPTER TWELVE

Political Assurance

"There's plenty of time—no need to start overdoing it," Roger pleaded with Marela.

The room around them was crowded. High elegant ceilings and brightly painted walls surrounded Marela and Roger. Everyone wore evening gowns and suits. Polished, click clack shoes that snapped across the floors with every step.

The Chancellor had not arrived. Everyone was buzzing loudly about how in 40 years since the Restoration he never had any opponents until now. Most were fascinated with Roger as if he were a newly discovered species of animal and others spoke in somber tones as if he were gravely ill.

"We need to get you introduced to every group at this ball," insisted Marela. "It doesn't matter if it's the first event—we may not ever see these people again."

That sounds like a drag. I don't think I'm as social as she thinks I can be.

Roger's palms were sweaty and his knees felt shaky. Marela thrived in this environment. She was talking away, shaking hands, smiling and delivering the message she and Roger had agreed upon before attending the event.

"Something needs to be done to prevent unnecessary lives being lost to inquiries," Marela said forcefully. "The Prelican Party has made a lot of positive changes for our society. They've gotten us this far. However, the Novolica of tomorrow will need to be different. Being able to ease the number of inquiries and maybe even eliminate them doesn't negate all the progress they've made."

She smiled widely as she spoke and Roger nodded accordingly alongside her.

"I can't tell if we are winning them over," Roger whispered once they were out of hearing distance from the last group. "Will they actually support us? I mean, do they actually think we have a shot at winning?"

"Well, no one seems particularly shocked or appalled at what we are saying. Our messaging as to not directly attack the Prelicans has certainly been received well. It should also make any impromptu inquiries for us less likely in the near future."

"The reactions from the mine workers were so different. They let Charly know almost immediately where they stood on the subject as he spread the word for me."

"Mhm, maybe they are worried about how the Chancellor will react upon arrival if he's informed they've publicly decided to support you instead. Though it seems like it's becoming less certain he'll actually show up."

After some time had passed and most people had left, a tall slender woman approached them. She had a long pointed nose and a serious look on her face as if something foul smelling was circling around the room. Her hair was fiery red and eyes as green as an open pasture. As she got closer, one of her arms stretched out toward their direction. Roger reached out but with a brief swipe, she turned directly toward Marela.

"I am Christen Yanes, public relations director for the Office of the Chancellor," she said sharply.

Her every breath commanded respect. Roger tried hard to swallow. Marela's face showed a puzzled expression.

"Marela de Nichols, campaign manager for Roger Aimes. Will the Chancellor be making an appearance tonight?" Marela replied while taking Christen's outstretched hand.

Christen put a hand down forcefully onto her hip.

"Chancellor Prumpt has been here the entire time," she smirked. "In the private lounge, separated from the main event. That portion is invitation only. None of the constituents there will be coming over to the lower party here. However, we were all buzzing about the two of you and the position you've taken. Therefore, I couldn't help but come meet you myself. Given that our event will be ending soon, I figured this was an opportune moment to stop by."

Marela and Roger were dumbfounded.

"Now no need to get all discouraged. We are still early in this—keep doing what you are doing."

Her smirk tightened. Marela put forth her best effort to remove any sense of worry on her face.

"We are very confident things will end in our favor," she forced with a high uplift of her chin.

Christen raised an eyebrow. "Hmmph," she grunted loudly. Then she turned on her heel, and left the room.

"She must have been trying to scare us or something," Roger said after she disappeared.

"I don't think so—it was almost like she wanted to see who she would be working for in the future," responded Marela. She looked oddly happy about the interaction, showing a big smile.

"How can you be so sure?"

"A hunch, I guess. She didn't need to come down here and speak to us at all. I'm also sure this is probably frowned upon behavior for someone part of the Chancellor's staff. I'm assuming she would have to work with any new person who was elected to keep her career."

"Well, she was definitely right about the event ending. Look around—everyone is clearing out. What do you say we call it a night?"

They both agreed and walked toward the exit.

~

The next day, Roger and Marela spent hours discussing every little detail about the initial opening event. Whom they spoke with, what was discussed, did that conversation help or hurt them, who they didn't get a chance to talk with they should've and on and on. Most importantly, they discussed why the Chancellor had a private event setup on the side.

"It doesn't make any sense," Roger said. "Why wouldn't he want to meet face to face? I thought for sure he'd want to try and scare me from challenging him or threaten me. I bet all of his followers were at his event which proves why our conversations went so easily."

Marela pondered this and Roger could tell she was as confused as him.

"Why the secrecy?" she responded after a few seconds. "I mean, we've gone over the procedures about a hundred times now." She pulled out her handheld and flicked a message upward from the tiny screen after scrolling. The message read:

RESTORATION OFFICIAL: FAIR LEGISLATIVE PROCESS ANY INDIVIDUAL THAT MAY FIND FAULT IN THE CURRENT LEADERSHIP OF NOVOLICA MAY SUBMIT THEIR NAME FOR A FULLY LEGAL AND JUST OPPOSITION PROCESS TO ENSURE SOUND LEADERSHIP AND FAIR PRACTICES IN THE REPUBLIC. THE PROCESS MILESTONES WILL FOLLOW ONCE THE CHALLENGING CANDIDATE'S IDENTITY HAS BEEN CONFIRMED:

FORMAL INTRODUCTION EVENT INCLUDING CHALLENGING CANDIDATES AND CURRENT LEADERSHIP TO DISCUSS PROCESS AND PROVIDE QUESTIONING

PUBLIC FACING ANNOUNCEMENT OF ELIGIBLE CHALLENGING CANDIDATES TO CURRENT LEADERSHIP

PUBLIC HEAD TO HEAD DEBATE BETWEEN CHALLENGING CANDIDATES AND CURRENT LEADERSHIP

ELECTRONIC HANDHELD POLLING SYSTEM ACTIVATED AND

SENT TO EVERY CITIZEN OF NOVOLICA TO CONFIRM PARTICIPA-
TION OF THE CHALLENGING CANDIDATE

UPON CONFIRMATION OF EACH CHALLENGING CANDIDATE
RECEIVING AT LEAST 20%, AN INQUIRY MUST BE COMPLETED
AT A PUBLIC SETTING IN WHICH CASE BOTH THE CHANCEL-
LOR AND THE CHALLENGING CANDIDATE WILL BE REQUIRED TO
SUCCESSFULLY PASS THE INQUIRY TO MOVE FORWARD

THE POLLING SYSTEM WILL REMAIN LIVE AND ACTIVE UN-
TIL THE PERMANENCE VOTE IN WHICH CASE EACH CANDIDATE
MUST MAINTAIN AT LEAST A 20% POPULARITY RATING TO CON-
TINUE THE PROCESS

ADDITIONAL DEBATES CAN BE SCHEDULED UPON AGREEMENT
OF CHALLENGING CANDIDATES AND CURRENT LEADERSHIP

TIME LIMIT NOT EXCEEDING 6 MONTHS AFTER THE CONFIR-
MATION OF THE CHALLENGING CANDIDATES FOR THE PERMA-
NENCE VOTE TO BE HELD VIA ELECTRONIC HANDHELD

CHALLENGING CANDIDATES AND CURRENT LEADER MAY NOT
PARTICIPATE IN THE PERMANENCE VOTE

BASED ON PERMANENCE VOTE RESULTS, THE ELECTORATE IS
TO BEGIN THEIR ROLE EXACTLY 30 DAYS FROM DATE OF PER-
MANENCE VOTE

ADDITIONAL GUIDELINES: PROCESS IS REQUIRED TO BE
TRANSPARENT THROUGHOUT FOR ALL CHALLENGING CANDI-
DATES AND CURRENT LEADERSHIP. NO PROSPECTIVE LEADER
IS PERMITTED TO ALTER OR HINDER THE AFOREMENTIONED
PROCESS IN ANY WAY. DUE PROCESS IS CRITICAL TO THE SUC-
CESS OF THE NATION AND FAIRNESS ACT ENACTED BY THE RES-
TORATION MOVEMENT. CITIZEN SUPPORT CAN BE WITHDRAWN
FROM ANY CHALLENGING CANDIDATE UP UNTIL THE PERMA-
NENCE VOTE. THE REMAINING CHALLENGING CANDIDATES
MUST HAVE AT LEAST 20% SUPPORT IN ORDER TO PARTICIPATE
IN THE PERMANENCE VOTE FOR OFFICE. FOR ANY QUESTIONS
OR CONCERNS THROUGHOUT THE PROCESS OR FOR ANY OF

THESE GUIDELINES YOU CAN CONTACT A RESTORED NATION, INC'S FRONT OFFICE.

"It's all here like we discussed. I think you could argue how things went yesterday weren't transparent. I mean we were completely blind-sided and told nothing about the event. Let alone the fact that there was an entirely separate private event for the Chancellor and his cronies."

Roger paced the room.

"Well, maybe we could make the case. But I am the only challenging candidate that we know of so far."

Marela looked disapproving.

"Ok—I am most likely the only challenging candidate. That means our word may mean very little without anyone else corroborating our claims. In that case, I guess the only thing we can do is discuss a strategy for the public announcement event in three days. I want to make sure I have a good speech ready."

"Yes," said Marela, "this could be your best chance to speak to everyone about why you are running. If the Chancellor does not agree to any head-to-head debates before the confirmation, it will be tougher for us."

"Do you really think he wouldn't? I mean, people love listening to him, right? What's he got to lose?"

"He has a lot more to lose than you. THAT we can be sure of. There's no telling what he would do to make this an easy victory for himself."

They both nodded. Their plan was sound, and they were going to execute on every tactic they could think of.

For the next three days they continued to plan. Roger worked on a speech, reciting it to Marela and Charly. Charly never gave any suggested changes but instead hooted loudly at every word he spoke.

"Sounds like you're about to whip the Chancellor all the way through the capitol and take his place!"

Charly agreed to keep rallying the workers at the mine to support him.

The morning of the public announcement, Roger made sure to wear the most sophisticated outfit he had. His long sleeved, black buttoned tunic complemented his silky black trousers and silvery socks.

He stepped over to the mirror in the corner of his room and admired his fit.

Wow, I barely recognize myself.

He read over his speech once more.

There better be an e-reader present. Memorizing all this definitely won't end well.

"My name is Roger Aimes…" he spoke aloud "the people I've lost and those that have been taken from us due to inquiries…"

aaand finish with high energy. No need to try and attack the system directly. Just show them there is another way to live outside of mentir screenings.

With a quick swipe of his finger his handheld flashed the time in front of him. 08:50. They had just under three hours to get to Leiton City where the event would be held. Roger walked into the main sitting area of the pod where Marela was checking her hair in front of the hub in mirror mode. Roger's breath was pulled from him and he felt engulfed in a warm fuzzy haze of bliss.

She… she's so beautiful.

She had on an emboldening black blazer with pointed tips at the shoulders. Her long wavy hair had been pulled up into a tight round bun encircled with a braid perfectly angled behind her head. She looked determined and her confidence gave Roger purpose.

"Hey, are you ready?" he asked her with a look of amazement.

She turned slowly and glanced at him, picking up on the look of awe.

She smiled at him and responded, "Yes. I like your idea of taking the shiloh after all. I would not want my wind bike to ruin all of my hard work this morning."

Roger stuck out his arm in a sideways motion, allowing Marela to grab hold. Once she had latched on, he ushered her out of the pod in a formal manner and they strode down the passway arm in arm to the shiloh station. A few people stopped and stared. They received a few half smiles and curious looks.

"Why are you both dressed so nicely on this boring new day? What's the occasion?" a stranger yelled at them from a distance.

They kept moving without giving an answer.

In less than an hour, I'll be changing Novolica for good.

"Twenty percent," Roger chanted under his breath. Twenty percent is all he would need to challenge the Chancellor's rule and end inquiries once and for all.

After disembarking the Shiloh in Leiton City, Roger pulled his handheld out and activated the locator. Within seconds, there was a transparent map floating out in front of them showing two blinking dots, guiding them.

The air was humid with a light breeze that whisked across their faces. As they approached the Renaissance building, they noticed a large crowd gathering. People moved about and chatted excitedly about someone who would be openly challenging the Chancellor. The Renaissance Building looked like a tall fortress. It was shaped like a dome and surrounded on all sides by menacing statues of Novolica's Prelican fighters from the Restoration War. They were all in fierce poses holding weapons with distinctly carved eyes and ferocious expressions.

Roger and Marela went to the side entrance of the building where they could see a security checkpoint. Christen Yanes' face stood out above the others huddled around the barriers. Once they had gotten closer, Christen connected with Marela's gaze and walked toward them.

Oh no, what does she want?

She greeted them curtly and ushered them through. Piercing eyes watched Roger intently as he crossed the slider and moved through the long corridor.

To his left and right there were people moving about the building with laser focus. Everyone was working with a purpose. Capture crews moved large moment freezing devices back and forth. Journalists were configuring their oversized handhelds specifically used for recording interviews with both their eyes and fingers glued to the screen.

Marela pointed out another group of statues. As they moved closer, they could see each sculpture was of the same person—Chancellor Prumpt. He looked stern, staring down at onlookers with a devilish smirk and commanding posture. A cold chill ran down Roger's spine.

As they approached the end of the corridor, he could see a path to their left leading out to the front lawn that had two lecterns set up. Instead of moving in that direction, Christen ushered them into a small room. Once the slider rotated in behind them, she looked at Marela again.

"Here is where he can get ready. Once the ceremony commences, someone will come to escort him outside. You can follow me now into the communal area where the Chancellor's team will be spectating the event."

She turned a side eye over to Roger and said in a lower tone, "I don't want any surprises—so keep it short."

Without saying anything else, she turned and led Marela out with her. Roger pulled out his handheld to rehearse. He paced while imagining himself saying the speech aloud and changing his voice.

"We owe it to ourselves... for the sake of our loved ones and friends in the community," he recited. He swiped left on the handheld to move the speech.

Eight minutes until the ceremony starts.

A voice coming from the next room leaked to Roger. He listened intently. Not one—

two voices. One of the voices sounded light and airy. They were swiftly cut off by the other speaker that sounded burly and dry.

That's the Chancellor! I've heard that voice way too many times not to recognize it. It sounds like he's upset with the other person about something.

He discreetly leaned in and pressed his ear directly to the metallic wall separating the two rooms.

"Did you pull his profile already?"

"Well we have been attempti—"

"DAMMIT, it's a simple question, I need a simple answer, Jameson. You should have had this ready weeks ago when the prick first submitted himself. We were supposed to blow this up before the public got a chance to validate him as a candidate. Now it's the day of the announcement and you're telling me you still have NOTHING. If he makes it past today, this bullshit is on you!"

What the hell?

The Chancellor's voice sounded combative and riled but his tone was oddly casual. It seemed like this was a normal conversation for him.

Are they really talking about me? Are they trying to sabotage me so soon?

A moment passed and he heard the voice of Jameson continue.

"The probability of him making it past the validation is dubious at best. Twenty percent of Novolica's citizens equates to two hundred million people. Our latest politrackers show that most people fully support you, Chancellor Prumpt, and the system we have successfully run for the past few decades. It looks like it's time for us to head out to the lectern."

The slider to Roger's room started to rotate. He spotted the nearest chair and quickly hopped over to it before the slider could open fully. A short and stocky man with thick glasses hanging low on a long pointed nose now appeared. The small amount of hair he had left was hugging the front most tip of his forehead. The man was holding what appeared to be an oversized handheld that he grasped tightly as he looked at Roger oddly.

Jeez, did he see me eavesdropping?

With a squeezing motion he activated his large screen handheld and a message started to appear up above the display for him and Roger to see.

"Mr. Aimes," the man said in a soft voice, "you have been summoned to the main stage to address the citizens of Novolica regarding your bid to become Chancellor. I will prescribe to you the sequence of today's events."

He read from the floating message that was now clearly visible to them both.

"As part of the Restoration Principles established on February 18th, 2086, this nation will adhere to the following process in order to establish a governing body for the freedom and fairness of all its citizens and those that would wish to become so. Any individual that wishes to assume the role of Chancellor need only to submit their name and data to the registration platform via handheld device.

"Once entered, the prospect must publicly announce their candidacy and garner twenty percent of the popular vote to become an official candidate for Chancellor. During which time, they will be required to maintain a twenty percent popularity status and undergo a public inquiry. The candidacy period will last up to or no longer than six months from the date of confirmation vote as decided upon by all participating parties.

"Today's event will feature a public address from each prospect for Chancellor, followed by an address from the Chancellor themself as they will be expected to continue with their role until a permanence vote is held and a new candidate is selected."

The greeter took a deep breath and looked up at Roger. His head was tilted as his mouth hung open.

"Any questions Mr. Aimes?"

Roger looked down, focusing intently on the back of his palms. He started to breathe the nervousness in the air, he felt his stomach swerve within his abdomen. With a deep, shaky exhale to try and steady himself and answered as calmly as he could.

"No questions," his voice cracked.

His palms were trembling.

"Very well then. Follow me."

Roger stood up with great effort and slowly followed the man through the slider.

"My apologies Mr. Aimes, Stacey Worchester by the way," the greeter said.

Roger shifted his body to his left to shake hands with Stacey as they walked side-by-side down a long hallway that warped into a fuzzy tunnel.

I can't see what's forwards or backwards in here. Ugh, it's like my stomach is trying to force its way out of my throat. So tight.

"This way Mr. Aimes," Stacey motioned to their left as he cut sharply down another hallway that led to an opening in the distance. A rumbling chatter grew louder as they approached. Roger bounced his shoulders up and down to try and relax himself.

Before he knew it, Stacey had stopped and motioned for Roger to continue forward out onto the main lectern. First he was greeted by a blinding sunlight that warmed his body. He looked to his right and saw the Chancellor sitting just across the way. The lectern was completely transparent with only a voice amplifier resting neatly on top. He noticed a large display floating in the distance that must have been used for exact reading. He quickly scanned the lectern for somewhere to dock his handheld as he knew that would allow him to put his speech up on the display for reading.

I'm finally here.

He moved his feet right up to the stand and was now facing a crowd of hundreds of people staring directly at him and him only. A sea of eager faces, fixated.

Why are there so many people here?

His arm started to shake as he slowly reached for his handheld.

Stay calm, just like you practiced, stay calm, it's time to make the nation safer for everyone.

Roger placed the handheld into the empty slot in the middle of the stand and it immediately lit up. With a few swipes of his index finger, his speech was now displayed on the large floating screen that no one but him could see.

As he was about to speak, he opened wide and sucked in air from the bottom of his stomach—when he heard a loud *TAP TAP*. Then he felt something poke him in the back. He turned around to see Marela hooking an audio device around his neck. She pressed firmly on a button on the side and suddenly Roger felt an electric surge pressing against his throat.

"Now everyone will be able to hear you—and they'll know you were meant to be here."

She flashed him a quick smile and retreated to where she had been standing. The flips in his stomach steadied. His tongue became moist once again. He turned and peered out into the crowd. With a firm clearing of his throat, Roger spoke.

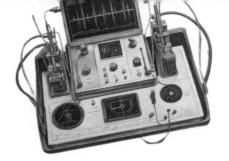

CHAPTER THIRTEEN

Deadly Confirmation

"People of Novolica, my name is Roger Allen Aimes.

"I am here today because there is something that is crushing our society. It's been eating at us from the inside out. A deadly sickness that has been diagnosed with absolutely no hope of being cured. A leech that has fed off the ones we love for forty years. We go about our everyday lives, afraid. Afraid this sickness will come for us at any time. We've all felt the cold unforgiving grasp of the mentir system. Those deadly machines clenched upon our wrists. For far too long we've sat by and walked willingly to our deaths. For this is the mandate that has been forced upon us.

"I'm here to tell you today, there is another way. By supporting me as your new Chancellor, my only objective is to remove the mentir screening laws from Novolica's governing documents—FOREVER. No longer will you be afraid to share your story. No longer will you fear being your true self. No longer will you have to identify the remains of someone you love for a death that met them much too soon. A friend, a coworker, a sister… a … a mother."

Roger held back the tears that began swelling in his eyes.

"Today, we stand together. We embrace the best parts of our nation, and we reconcile those pieces that hold us back from true freedom."

Raucous applause boomed loudly. The crowd was embracing Roger. "RECONCILE," shouted someone from the audience. Others followed and began chanting along with them. "RE-CON-CILE, RE-CON-CILE, RE-CON-CILE."

"I want to bring about the society that Novolica could become. One that would be fair while maintaining the principles we all hold dear to our hearts." Roger's voice grew stronger. **"This is my official announcement as a prospective candidate. Support me and together we will reconcile Novolica!"** More cheers thundered loudly, shaking the ground.

Twenty percent, please I only need twenty percent. Please let them believe in me.

Mr. Worchester came to usher Roger away from the lectern. As he turned, he caught a glimpse of one of the foulest scowls he had ever seen on another human being. Chancellor Prumpt was glaring at him full of rage.

What will he say? He looks furious. As long as it ends with him put away for good.

Someone else had moved to the lectern with a large display handheld similar to the one that Mr. Worchester had.

"Citizens, we will now be opening the polling system."

All of the noise from the crowd was drowned in an instant.

It's happening. Will I make it?

Though the crowd continued shouting, mouths moving, hands clapping, everyone was now completely inaudible. Just a distant buzzing. Time was frozen. Roger felt his own handheld vibrate lightly. He looked down at it. There on the screen in big bold print was his name.

Candidate Polling Interface: Activated

Roger Allen Aimes ---------- Approval Percentage

Select "Thumbs Up" or "Thumbs Down"

SUBMIT

Roger's hands were shaking. He tried hard to control himself. Slowly, deliberately he slid his finger across the tiny screen. It was time.

It starts with me. No one should ever feel the pain I've felt again. Ma, the pain Marela felt from Briyano. Everything Juss has been through. After I vote for myself, I'll see the results. I'll see exactly what everyone thinks of me. Am I even capable of leading these people? All of Novolica. They can all see me. If I fail, I've failed millions of people.

Roger looked up at the hub capturers.

Everyone can see me. On the expressways, in their pods, at work. My fate is in their hands. Sunny! He's in a director's office right now. Contemplating if he believes I can be the next Chancellor. He helped me get here, despite what that asshole said about him, he's always been a Prumpt supporter. Charly, he believes in me. Marela, she believes in me. Now I have to believe in myself.

BEEP. He chose the thumbs up, SUBMITTED. Now he could see a rapidly increasing percentage showing beside his name.

14… 15…17, the percentage number beside his name flickered. His approval rating continued, 16…18…19…17…

There must be people changing their answer.

It rose steadily again 19… 21…23…24.

The crowd now came back into view. Their applause filled the area. A loud celebratory trumpet noise wailed.

The announcer was back at the lectern. "ROGER ALLEN AIMES HAS BEEN CONFIRMED AS A CANDIDATE FOR CHANCELLOR."

Roger's heart leapt. Marela ran to him and hugged him. The announcer and everyone in the waiting area looked to him in awe as he and Marela embraced one another. One who did not look over, smile, or clap was the Chancellor himself. Despite all the commotion, he remained unnervingly composed.

Stacey, now standing alone before the audience, turned in the direction of the Chancellor and motioned for him to come to the lectern. He stood up strongly. He was wearing a thick gray long sleeve tunic with hefty cuffs and a loose neck. His dark brown pants were embellished with blue rhinestones. He was shorter than Roger but more rounded in the midsection and much more square in the face. As he approached the lectern, his hands met each other in the middle. Silence fell over the crowd. Roger's whole body clenched. The Chancellor had no notes. He swiped his hand swiftly under the stand, causing a small sound grabber to appear from the top. He leaned in to speak.

"People of Novolica. I address you today as my fellow citizens. As we have stood strong in arms together to protect the values we hold sacred within this amazing country. We are one people. However, there is a small minority that have decided to betray our nation, that want to see us thrown into chaos. These imbeciles want to see our way of life destroyed, our pods ransacked, and our families torn apart. They have no respect for honor and truth. They'd rather we live in a lawless society with no government and no safety.

"This jackoff is the voice of this reckless group that wants to stand in the way of our way of eternal prosperity and safety. You being able to sleep sound at night, knowing you are safe and your children having the opportunity to grow up and be something is being threatened by the challenger and anyone who chooses to follow him. They want you to be watched over by someone with no life goals, no real plan, no clue whatsoever how to lead you. A low-level laborer hauling machine parts for a living. Someone from a broken family with no friends and no love. A loner piece of shit that has forgotten, too young to even remember the struggles that we have overcome. The lives we have saved and the families that can now put food on their tables due to the Restoration.

"We must preserve our way of life at any cost. Make no mistake, without these processes in place that are built to protect us, we are all vulnerable. Our survival and sustainability is held together by the principles we as a nation established by way of the Restoration. I offer myself as your continued Chancellor to uphold the foundation that has protected you and led this great nation to become what it is today. Thank you, my people."

With a wave of his hand he swiftly moved away from the stage area and out of sight. His staff followed him. Loud cheering accompanied his exit.

Roger clasped his hands together nervously. *I didn't think he would just out and attack me personally that way. Everyone's cheering him on. It's like I wasn't just up there.*

Roger looked back at the poll. His rating had dropped four points, to twenty-one percent.

He looked over at Marela. Her face was scrunched as she stared intently at her handheld.

Stay above twenty, please stay above twenty.

He tried to take deep breaths.

I know why I'm here. I'm doing what needs to be done. To save lives for the betterment of everyone. It will be ok.

He sat up straight and tucked his handheld away.

He returned his gaze toward Marela. She lifted her chin back at him, smiling. Stacey got up to report the final approval ratings and announced the next event. A public mentir screening, followed by an address from both candidates.

"Only a month until the next event," Marela beamed happily as everyone left.

Roger and Marela weaved through small crowds to head home.

"It won't be easy. After seeing how much the crowd enjoyed your presence, I'm sure the Chancellor will try to sabotage you. Did you hear how he spoke today? He is furious at the thought of someone challenging him and getting support. There's no telling how far the Prelican party will go to keep their leader in power and make sure things continue to operate how they want them."

"It couldn't be that bad. If they didn't want anyone challenging them, why would they include it in the Reformation documents?"

"HAH! They can try to put on the show that they care about the good of the people and that ruling is done by the people. But we know that they are the ones making all the decisions and have been for decades. The fact that no other leader has ever been selected proves that they want things to stay the way they are. We have to be prepared for what comes next. The next event is a public inquiry. When you become Chancellor, you'll have to do these frequently until you can change the mandate. So best get used to this sensation now. Millions of people watching you an inch away from being executed for mentirring. Chancellor Prumpt has done this thousands of times he'll have an advantage."

Marela was so deep in her strategizing efforts, she hadn't noticed the large grin that had crept over Roger's face.

"Does getting killed in public make you happy?" she asked him inquisitively.

"Absolutely not. But I couldn't help but notice you said WHEN I become Chancellor."

He gazed at her. As they fell into each other's eyes, their chatter became softer. Each more enamored with the other in hopes of changing the world together.

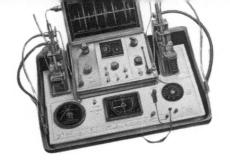

CHAPTER FOURTEEN

Let It Slide

The day before the public inquiry, Roger's approval rating had increased to thirty-one percent. Novolica was embracing his ideals. Marela and Rogers sat much closer to one another than usual. Surfing the hub channels to see the latest news about the campaign.

"Roger Aimes is a legitimate candidate," said one reporter. "Yes, indeed he has qualities of a future chancellor."

Another rep replied, "If you ask me, his campaign manager Marela de Nichols is the one calling the shots. Without her, this all falls apart. He's too unqualified for this type of position."

"Well either way, he's got to pass the public inquiry tomorrow to reach the final vote."

Roger looked away from the screen and down at his handheld. "My device says Prumpt just gave another speech. You may have to switch to the other channel."

Marela picked up her handheld and moved quickly across the tiles until she saw the Chancellor's face. He was surrounded by a gang of Prelicans who looked on with rapt attention as he began his speech.

"Our nation has been restored from the piece of shit it once was. Idiots running everything into the ground. Absolutely no one could be trusted and the old leaders were nothing more than scam artists!

Con men who wanted to suck all the wealth and happiness from us. They came in here and took what belonged to us. They made a mockery of our nation and pissed all over our society. We said enough was enough. We came in and put a stop to those motherfuckers. We the people decided that it was time for a change. And look at how far we've come today.

"Novolica is now a place we can be proud to call home. Free from the burden of leeches and heretics. Had our Prelican government not established rule and set the precedent for success here, we would all be wiped out. Eaten from the inside out, ceased to exist. Any change in leadership now would put all the work we've done at risk. Unless you want to leave behind 40 years of progress and stabilization, withdraw your support from this asshole parading himself like he can lead this nation. Punish anyone you see that is supporting that ignorant son of a bitch. We all see what he truly is and that is not someone we want to be here."

The crowd cheered loudly.

A cold shiver ran down Roger's spine. He trembled in place, hooking his hands around his arms.

"Don't be so alarmed. It's harsh words, but I warned you this would happen," Marela said soothingly.

"I just don't know how to respond to this. I've never spoken to the guy but it's like he absolutely hates me. He's asking for people to get violent against me and my supporters."

"Every action has an equal and opposite reaction. We aren't doing this because it's fun or easy. We are taking a stand to stop the mentirring system. There are millions of people who feel the same way we do. We are doing this for them."

Roger nodded in agreement.

"Off to the public inquiry I go tomorrow then."

～

When Roger arrived at the Renaissance building the next morning, he felt jittery. He was sweating profusely as he was escorted to his prep room.

Ok, we are here. Just practice the speech. After the inquiry is over, I'll be addressing the people. It'll be ok.

He paced the familiar room and began rehearsing his speech and how to respond to questioning. His abdomen area was turning in circles. He paused to collect himself.

Calm down, deep breaths. Just breathe.

In the silence, he heard the slider in the next room over rotating and footsteps moving about. The familiar gritty sounding voice began yelling. Roger brought his ear to the wall to listen in.

"Let's hurry and get this over with already. How much time until we get started?"

"Um—it looks like we've got maybe–"

"I don't want to hear any um's or maybes, Jameson! Be specific dammit."

There was a pause. The second voice then spoke up once more, in a manner much calmer and quieter than that of the Chancellor.

"We have exactly seventeen minutes. It looks like your inquiry will be first, followed by your address to the people. Then your opponent will be subject to his inquiry after another confirmation that his approval rating has remained above the requirement."

"How the hell did our inquiry get scheduled before his?"

"You insisted on this change last week, sir."

"This is all going to hell. It should be my address first, then his inquiry—that way he wouldn't have the chance to give an address. Now I'll have to go on with it. You better have my X5 in place. If I get bled out on stage what I have to say doesn't matter anymore."

"Of course sir, we had one of the Prelican operating machines sent here three days ago to replace the factory model the Renaissance center keeps on hand."

"Have we made sure he won't be able to use the X5? I don't give a damn if he gets cut."

"Yes of course sir, however it would look suspicious using two different mentir detectors out in front of everyone. Him receiving the benefit of using one of the Prelican machines far outweighs the risk of—"

"I get it, I'm smarter than you Jameson—I very well comprehend the situation. I just don't want that prick anywhere near our gear."

"Sir, it's time to head out. I just received a beep from Worchester to come to the front."

There was a shuffling noise, then a loud *CLINK CLANK* which must have been another storage compartment being opened. The sound of the main slider rotating to let the men exit out into the hallway.

Roger found himself frozen. He tried to force himself back away from the wall but his body shut down on him.

What did I just hear? The Chancellor talking about a special "Prelican only" machine being used for mentir detecting. "I don't give a damn if he gets cut". Why would he say something like that? Wouldn't the Prelican device do the same thing to him if he was found mentirring? How could he only attribute the possibility of being caught for mentirring to a jig that's not his? Something isn't adding up.

"There's no way. Could it be? Are…they really able to—"

Roger's speaking aloud was halted at the sound of the room slider opening.

"There you are Mr. Aimes," shouted Stacey with a large grin on his face.

Roger said nothing but gazed loosely over the forehead of Stacey out into nothingness. He was gripping his chin tightly, mind racing.

"Is your address all set and ready to go? I'm sure you will have some excellent things to say once you've passed your mentir screening I presume?"

Hearing this jolted Roger back to the present. "I—I do have my address, but—"

Roger made a motion toward his handheld. He had completely forgotten what he was going to say after the inquiry.

"Well done!" cut in Stacey. "We will have to head there now, they are about to clip the Chancellor in to complete his inquiry. Follow me."

As they moved through the threshold, Roger felt his feet go numb. His body iced over. He pondered his options.

I've got to expose Prumpt. There is no way he's getting away with this. I won't stand for it. I have to tell everyone what I know.

Stacey eyed him consolingly while still moving ahead.

"One could argue the hard part is over," he forced himself to say with a half grin showing. "You've already gotten the approval rating. The speech today after your inquiry will not be nearly as intense. In fact, you could choose to not speak at all in front of the crowd in case you feel in shock or something."

This didn't register with Roger. He was too occupied thinking about how he was going to inform the public of this devastating news. Stacey shrugged, giving up on trying to make him feel better.

As they approached the lawn, banging and shouting noises emanated from the crowd. He could now see the Chancellor and his main support staff. His inquiry had been completed and he was now addressing the crowd. Though from this distance, Roger couldn't hear what he was saying. Roger could see a faint shiny glimmer of gold a few steps from where the Chancellor was standing.

That must be the faulty X5 jig he used to pass his screening.

As he got closer, the noises of the speaker and audience became clearer. Before he reached the seating area behind the podium, the hairs on the back of his neck stood straight up. Nearly all of the eyes of both the onlookers and chancellor supporters were now staring angrily, directly at him.

What did he say now? Has the Chancellor come up with some unidentified clause in the proclamation of becoming the leader of the nation? Was there something I overlooked? Have I already lost my chance to change Novolica and stop the inquiries once and for all?

A large lump formed in the middle of his throat. He continued to hobble awkwardly toward the waiting area. He locked eyes with Marela, who seemed very off. She didn't appear angry like everyone else, but she looked deeply saddened. Her eyes were starting to water. Roger approached her, trying to ignore everyone staring at him still.

"What happened?"

Before she could answer, he was addressed directly by Prumpt himself on the audio enhancer.

"Now they all know, Aimes. Did you really think your dark past wouldn't catch up to you? The horrible things you've done, you thought you could bury it and no one would find out? I have a daughter you bastard and women are not part of this great nation to be used and discarded," he said with a sharp vindictive tone.

Roger's heart started pounding. He gently reached for Marela's hand. In an instant she pulled it away.

No, not here, not now. I have to tell her what the Chancellor has been doing to pass his inquiries. I have to tell everyone. Roger turned to the podium abruptly.

I can't let this happen. I know the truth about him. The time is now.

He made a move toward the podium, fists now clenched. Before he could take two steps forward he felt two big bodies collapse against him. Both his arms were now being gripped tightly and a third person had wrapped him around his waist from behind and was pulling him backward. He struggled to claw his way out. The weight of the three large men forcing him backward empowered him even more. Two more steps toward the lectern.

Just reach the audio grabber. I have to tell them.

The Chancellor moved off the platform to put distance between the two of them.

There it is. Just a few more steps. If I yell now, it'll pick up the sound.

"HIM," Roger cried out in the struggle to move. "HE'S A FAKE!"

Another body had now pummeled into them. This one took the front of Roger and put himself between him, the audience, and the Chancellor. This one was not messing around. He rounded on Roger and dug his large fist deep into his abdomen.

Roger doubled over as every breath he had in his body was forced out of him all at once. He gasped to find his breath again but before he could another blow came hard at him. This time on the back of his head. He turned to look around and saw the tip of an elbow come down on him.

And then darkness. He felt a numbing sensation creep slowly over his body followed by fingers around his neck. Then, weightlessness.

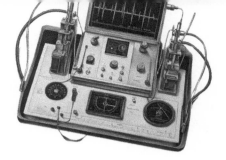

CHAPTER FIFTEEN

Topsy Turvy

"Where am I? What happened to me?" Roger croaked in his hospital bed.

A sharp, throbbing pain pulsed in his head. He touched the large bandage around his forehead and brace around his neck. His vision was blurry as flashes of light gradually returned to him. There was a large hub in the room streaming information about animals. He was wearing a silk yellow gown. A thick needle stuck in his left arm and connected to an electronic feeder stopped him from moving freely. The nauseating odor of sanitizer filled his nostrils.

The large metallic screen in the front of the room read in big letters:
NURSE: STUMP, JAMES ERLICK.
PATIENT: AIMES, ROGER ALLEN, AGE: 28
AILMENT: HEAD TRAUMA.

Roger's stomach turned as he remembered what put him here. Goosebumps covered his shivering body.

"It must be seven degrees in here," he muttered.

He sat up as the slider rotated open.

What if this is some crazy hub rep? Should I pretend to be asleep?

He took a few deep breaths which made his head throb. A staff aide walked in carrying a small tray with a clear vile and a fresh gauze. He was abnormally pale with an oversized head. He had extremely wide-set eyes with a thick insect-like brow over them.

"Name's James, Mr. Aimes," said the aide.

He wore a dark blue buttoned tunic that had a handheld tucked in a shallow slit across the front. James came beside the bed and leaned over Roger to sit him upright.

He was wearing an old ticker on his wrist. Shining with a bulky, metallic looking frame. When Roger looked at it, a display of applications appeared in mid-air.

"Oop, sorry—much sorry considering that. It's temperamental, Mr. Aimes, muto muto temperamental. It's caught your eye, I see," grinned the aide. With a flick of his finger, he closed the options menu. Now it only showed the time. Roger tried to avert his eyes quickly.

"Why in the hell do you have that?" cried Roger, alarmed.

"Ahh so you believe the superstitions about these, huh? It is not true much at all not much true. There's no bad vibes with these like what people say. Seeing the time this way won't bring you to an early death. It actually much more so keeps you grounded. Don't worry much. How's your head feeling Sir? You took a muto muto crazy hit to your dome. Took a much bigger hit to your pride, bigger much at losing the run at Chancellor like that. Nope—no bandages to heal that one much."

So it really is over.

Roger grabbed his head and forced his eyes shut trying to tune out the throbbing.

"I got a much much needed dose for you right here Mr. Aimes, it should help much."

James gestured toward the vile and pulled an air injector from the slit with the handheld. He fixated on one end of the valve and propped his hand on the middle of Roger's face.

"Whoa, watch it."

His fingertips stunk of stale food and germ killer. He aggressively jerked Roger's head to one side causing his neck to pop. In an instant the air injector was positioned on his neck. James pushed it and sent a cold dose of painkiller through Roger's bloodstream.

Within seconds, he could already feel the ringing noise become fainter. Roger sank limply into the bed. James started unwrapping the bandage on Roger's head. In a circular motion he rotated his bony elbows, narrowly missing hitting him more than once.

After the bandage had been replaced, Roger spoke again.

"How long have I been here?"

"Nearly two days, Sir. Your much special friend has been worried much sick. I believe she is on her way back here now."

"Special friend?"

"Yes sir! Not much other way to say it Mr. Aimes, not much at all. She had all your information for us when you were brought in. But she was much insistent she is not your wife, no sir she told us much that. Not a domestic partner either though you both have the same pod location. Muto muto unique situation. I had to list her as that title so she could come and see you without restriction. She's been here hours at a time."

A smile crept over Roger's face. *I guess I still have my biggest supporter.*

"I think you will be able to leave tomorrow. Your wound should finish healing by tonight. That new protogel works wonders to get rid of nasty bruises like the one you had."

James looked at the ticker on his wrist. He flicked upward, showing the menu options again. Roger jerked his head back, leaning awkwardly out of the way of the device. James was amused by this and put it closer to Roger's face.

He flashed a deviously satisfied look before backing away from him and closing the menu.

"You could have been our new Chancellor, but you failed muto muto wildly. Why did you have to go and do that to the woman? You could be put in confinement, you know."

A sour taste welled up inside Roger's mouth. *What did the Chancellor say about me?*

"I sent my approval vote for you," continued James. "You were going up and up, past thirty percent. Then it much tanked and went down much and down. Much much down, no way to recover or continue. I saw it go below one percent and then the poll was closed once it was determined you would never get back to the necessary level. You didn't get much chance to speak."

James grabbed Roger's arm, startling him. They locked eyes.

"WHY, WHY did you go all crazy much? You could have had a chance to talk but you tried to attack the Chancellor. I have a relative in the mine rows here in Finca."

So I am back in Finca.

"She says she has never spoken to you but she has heard about you from other workers there. People there respect you. Many don't know what to believe now. They have never seen you shouting and try to attack someone,"

"I DID NOT TRY TO ATTACK HIM!" Roger was at his limit.

"I had not even heard what Prumpt said about me because I was coming from the waiting room. I was trying to tell everyone—I was hoping the sound analyzers would pick it up. The Chancellor, he…"

Roger hesitated.

"He—cannot be trusted," he forced.

James looked at him skeptically. "Well, seems like we cannot trust you much either Sir, going all crazy much like that."

With these last words, James gathered the items he had brought into the room and headed back out.

Roger felt hot. His heart was pounding in his chest.

James didn't believe anything I said. Of course he doesn't. There's no evidence of what I heard. No sound from what I was shouting. Everybody will think the same as James, I went crazy over this story from the Chancellor. I need Marela, she has to know the truth. Then we'll figure out how to tell everyone.

The slider of the room opened again.

Marela walked in with a confident stride. Her long curly hair swished around her neck. She was wearing a white blazer with a royal blue blouse and a black skirt. She found a chair nearby and pushed it beside Roger's bed. There she sat, staring directly at him. Completely still and silent with her arms folded.

Roger stared back, breathing loudly.

"I would never do that to a woman. I don't have it in me. What happened all those years ago, I used poor judgment, but in no way did I do anything wrong."

Roger paused. Seeing Marela's blazing stare unchanged, he continued.

"I met Monica a few days after I was first assigned to the mine rows. After we were assigned our careers, I wasn't sure if you and I would be able to reconnect. It was like I didn't have a chance to be with you. I thought about you every day and being away from you made me feel… lonely.

"When the mine row team invited me out, I took them up on their offer to clear my head. Monica was there with a few of her friends. We were chatting and we really hit it off. We separated from the group and went off alone. I—I remember it like it was yesterday. She offered to buy the next round and I agreed to stay longer. We were by the bar and she started signaling. I mean, every signal you could think of arm rubbing, leg grabbing, shoulder bumping together. I thought for sure she wanted to spend a night together.

"Halfway through the last round she asked if she could stay at my place. I agreed and so she grabbed my hand and pulled me outside. Together we headed back toward my pod. She was holding onto me so tightly, arms around my waist. I—I returned the affection. We both stumbled about, feeling the drinks we'd had. I felt excited and I didn't want to wait until we got back.

"We were walking by an old passway exit that led out onto a field. There were two abandoned buildings covering the exit from view of the main path. I ducked in between them and called out to her to follow me. It was dark, but I could see her stop—there was some hesitation but she followed me willingly.

"Once we were out of sight, I pushed her up against one of the buildings and we went at it. Completely falling all over each other. I tasted her lips, her tongue. Caressed her cheeks. We were right on top of one another smooching harder than I ever had. She grabbed me—strongly.

"I remember her grip so firm around the edges of my pants and pulling me as close to her crotch as she could. Then we heard a loud noise from the field. It sounded like someone was celebrating and we heard a group of footsteps on the main passway.

"She must have thought the group was cheering for us as some type of sick joke or that maybe I was going to trick her into letting other men have their way with her. I don't know—but she got startled and panicked. She completely lost it and all the affection was replaced with anger.

"I was caught off guard. She frantically jumped, screaming and throwing her hands at me in the dark, fighting me back. The group quickly came out of nowhere to see what was happening thinking someone was in danger. Once they arrived they saw me—shirt tattered and her lipstick smeared across my face—and Monica in tears, looking disheveled. Before they could ask any questions, she took off. The group alerted the authorities on a handheld and when they arrived, I told them what happened.

"Since the girl was nowhere to be found, no charges were brought against me. Though the group was sure I had attacked her and that I was going to try to take advantage of her had they not showed up. It turned out to be the worst night of my entire life.

"I never saw Monica again but I cannot forget her face. To this day, there's an open file in my name, I hear. That if she ever wanted to come forward and accuse me, she would be able to. At the risk of sending me to an institution."

"Did you get called in for an inquiry?"

With a heavy sigh, Roger broke eye contact with Marela for the first time.

"No, I didn't. I don't know why. I thought for sure someone from the group that reported it would submit my name. Of course I thought she might. I waited weeks and weeks, not able to sleep or hardly eat. But it never came.

"I told myself that I hadn't done anything wrong. But honestly, that never stuck well. Maybe she was so intoxicated, she couldn't remember my name or enough of what had happened to submit the inquiry. Hell, maybe even she fell during her quick exit and hit her head somewhere. Maybe she blacked out and doesn't have any recollection of what happened at all. Either way, for seven years, I never had to address it again. But somehow the Chancellor found out."

Marela had not interrupted Roger once. She sat there, still, and deliberately pondered everything he had said.

"It really is brilliant. He raised doubts about your character. The type of doubt that absolutely no one would stand for. You telling your side of the story would not have swayed many people and it definitely would not have kept you above the minimum required approval rate to go forward with your inquiry.

"But if you had been able to go forward with it, it would have been the perfect opportunity for you to prove your innocence. If the Chancellor is willing to take that kind of risk publicly to make sure you do not get a chance at taking his position, there is no telling what else he would do. The lengths he would be willing to go—"

"YOU ARE RIGHT," Roger blurted. "That's not even the worst of it—I've got to tell you something."

Marela cut in once more. "Does this have something to do with you shouting and going berserk about him being a fake? A fake—what exactly?"

Roger stiffened. Marela was completely fixated on him.

"He's been betraying Novolica this entire time. That bastard."

Roger's fists clenched tightly as he felt these words leave his mouth hot and with searing anger behind them.

"The mentir machines they use—Prumpt and his Prelican leaders—don't actually work."

"What? There's no… that's not possible," said Marela in a shaky voice.

"No—I think you of all people know that it is possible. It all makes sense now. You told me before that the X-series jigs used for public figures are different from the ones you build the algorithms for. And that they are even kept in a secret, approved access-only part of the building so no one ever sees the production of these machines or which ones are sent out.

"Prumpt's prep room at the Renaissance building was directly next to mine. I heard him tell his assistant that he needed to make sure his special X5 jig was ready and had been placed on the podium. This way there was no chance of him being found guilty of mentirring. I could hear it in his voice—he was dead serious. Not only did the prick admit that he couldn't be killed with his machine, he wanted to make sure that the machine assigned to me was different so I would receive the *be-ne-fit*.

"He was so upset when he found out that I would have been using his X5 too—because he knew the information he was about to tell everyone about me was not true. But he said it would all go to waste if I was allowed to go through with my inquiry."

Marela stood up. A look of shock spread across her face.

"I know—I couldn't believe it at first either," Roger said. "I've run it over in my head about a thousand times. He's been mentirring the entire time, through all of it. I bet it's easier for him and his cronies to keep pushing these inquiries on everyone considering they do not have to worry about being killed. It is a disgrace."

"I—I knew it, Marela said. "Well I always suspected it. The way that people in the office act, the small number of people that do have access to the mentir detectors only used for class 5 citizens. They are never seen chatting with anyone else or in common areas at work. You would never know who exactly they are and they never change roles nor do they recruit anyone into their jobs.

"I always thought it was strange how every other machine goes through the same process and procedures except for those. I've seen thousands of these things and not once have I ever even caught a glimpse of the ones I've seen the Chancellor or any eeeeelected official use on the hub," she said as she shook off a lewd gesture with her hand.

They looked at each other, eyes locked for what felt like hours. They were both deep in thought.

"How are we going to get it out?" asked Roger finally. "We've gotta expose him. But I'm not a candidate anymore. Without the twenty percent approval rating, there aren't any more events scheduled. No public meetings, no announcements. We've lost any chance we have at telling Novolica about this."

Marela put one hand on her left hip and leaned her head to one side.

"We haven't lost a damn thing. Everything we set out to do is far from over, boy. Don't you get it, Roger? Your name. Who you are, all of the support you had before that ridiculous story was said about you. You cannot be thrown away and kicked outside never to be remembered or heard from again. You are already a living legend!

"The people who supported you, they all want what we want. To end these inquiries once and for all. I promise you, absolutely—ABSOLUTELY NO ONE IS GOING TO DISMISS THE IDEA THAT THE PRELICANS HAVE BEEN CHEATING US THIS ENTIRE TIME. PEOPLE WE LOVE HAVE DIED! FRIENDS, FAMILY, COWORKERS. THERE IS NO WAY IN HELL THEY ARE GETTING AWAY WITH THIS ANY LONGER."

Her raised voice had nearly made Roger jump out of his gown. The hairs on his arms were standing straight up.

"It all sounds good," he answered. "But how do we do it? Where do we even start?"

Marela paced the room. Looking back at Roger she yelled, "Jolla! My friend from the academy. She operates her own hub network out of La Bajo. We can go there tomorrow. We'll tell her what you heard and record a segment she can start airing. Her station is mainly heard by citizens in La Bajo, but most of them detest the Prelicans already.

They will help us get the word out and recover your approval rating. I'm sure of it."

"I want to go now. But I guess I do need to recover more." He said this while grabbing his side.

"I think this could work. I have one question for you though."

He swallowed and looked at Marela closely.

"What will they do when they know we know?"

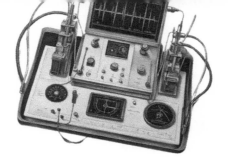

CHAPTER SIXTEEN

Every Ally Counts

La Bajo was cold and dry. Roger and Marela walked gingerly down the dilapidated passways, stepping carefully to avoid all the small holes. Snickers, small animals with overly large buck teeth, green beady eyes, and wiry black fur were responsible for the holes. Stepping into one would expose anyone to their long, razor sharp claws grabbing hold of you and leaving bloody scratch marks all over your feet and ankles.

"One of these caught hold of me once when I was a kid," Marela said casually as she hopped around the holes, pointing out a scurrying shadow. While she navigated with ease, Roger on the other hand had been taking each step slowly and deliberately to get around the holes.

"I couldn't walk for a month. My parents couldn't afford the latest treatment so I had to let it heal on its own."

That doesn't make me feel any better about walking. We should've found transportation. This is bananas. I wonder how these things survive in these conditions.

Roger pulled his jacket tighter around him looking up at the sky for a moment.

"Look out!" Marela shouted.

Roger refocused on the ground near his feet. He narrowly missed walking right into a large gaping burrow. Nestled inside was a family of snickers flashing.

"That would have been nasty."

Marela led him off the path toward a cluster of pods.

"Jolla lives right down this way."

This side route was much smoother than the passway. After a few minutes, they arrived at a large, luxurious looking pod with a dark blue dome shaped outer shell. They hurried toward the entrance. Marela swiped her handheld against the display panel beside the slider. After a few seconds, a woman appeared on the screen.

"MAREEEE DEAR, IT'S BEEN SO LONG! COME IN, COME IN," she said in an excited voice.

Her face disappeared from the display as the slider rotated open. Inside they faced a glass like material blocking their way. As they waited, the floor beneath sunk, lowering them under the pod. Roger stumbled before grabbing one of the rails beside him. After a few seconds, the floor came to a halt and the glass slider opened. A brightly smiling woman stood in its place. She wore a loose fitting blouse with sleeves that blossomed outward like flowers in bloom. She was widely shaped and even shorter than Marela. Her blonde hair, tinted with an array of colors stood frozen as she came forward with her arms outstretched toward Marela.

"Mareee amore, I am so glad you came."

She embraced Marela with a firm hug and nodded in Roger's direction.

She ushered them into the sitting area. There were two large cushioned chairs sitting side by side in front of an oversized hub covering the back wall and an enormous rotating table in the middle of the floor. Jolla plugged her handheld into the side of the table. She sat down as Roger and Marela followed.

After a few moments, the rotating table rose up revealing a compartment with mugs. Each mug had been filled with a sizzling, creamy liquid. Jolla took one of them and leaned back into her chair, legs crossed.

Roger and Marela also took a mug once the rotating compartment reached them. The table automatically closed its compartment and sank back into the floor. Jolla pulled her handheld from the side and stuffed it into the top of her blouse.

"You two have been busy. Thought you might have been the ones to get rid of that asshole."

"So did we," said Marela with a smile back at her friend. "But we didn't think he would resort to mentirring to get his way. We should have known but—"

"Hold up, are you telling me that story about Roger wasn't true? We all saw him go crazy when he heard his dirty secret had been spilled. Looked like he was going to tear the whole place down until those Prellies knocked him out cold."

"I had no idea what he had said about me when I arrived there," Roger insisted. "What I found out and why I kind of lost it… is the same reason why we're here to see you."

Roger looked anxious. Without acknowledging what he had said, Jolla turned back toward Marela.

"Why are you even still with him? Someone that would do something like that to a woman. I told you, you should have come alone."

Roger jerked his head abruptly and squinted intensely at Marela. Ignoring him, she looked back at Jolla with the softest unchanged expression.

"I would not be here if I thought this trip was pointless. Nor would I be anywhere near him if I thought that story was true. We talked about it and it didn't happen as the Chancellor said. I know it won't change your mind. The only thing that matters is I believe it and we're here to tell you why you *should NOT* believe anything the Chancellor says."

Jolla uncrossed her top leg and sat upright leaning in toward Marela. Roger's heart was pounding.

Ok, I'll let them talk. No problem at all.

Marela continued. "I was sitting in the executive spectator section during the Chancellor's address. It's true that Roger was not outside yet while he was talking. The moment he appeared was the moment the Chancellor turned and addressed him directly. Otherwise Rog would've probably sat down with me and waited for him to finish. I wasn't exactly sure what set him off, but now I know. Their preparation areas are located beside one another and separated by a thin lining. He overheard the Chancellor and his aide talk about bringing in his rigged X5 jig."

She paused for a moment. Marela spoke slowly and over emphasized every word.

"He said that as long as his special machine was in place, he did not have to worry about being found guilty of mentirring—ever."

Jolla sat motionless. Her gaze at Marela had softened. There was a brief quiver in her bottom lip. After a few seconds Marela snapped her fingers loudly.

"JOLLA."

"I heard you—let me think."

She folded her arms in front of her and focused her gaze once more at the two of them.

"This isn't the first time someone has made an accusation like this. We get people coming in claiming that everything is rigged. Prelicans have special codes or inhibitors put in their bodies to prevent mentir machines from detecting them. One scenario is as good and as implausible as the next.

"You expect me to believe because this one here might have overheard something that this is any better or more concrete than the rest of them? Where's the proof? Evidence... recording... something that won't make me look like an absolute fool. Or worse, get me brought in for questioning and sliced."

A stain of contempt flashed briefly across Marela's face. One of her eyebrows raised.

"So you don't believe us then—is that what it is? After everything that we've been through together."

"You don't understand," Jolla interjected with a click of her tongue. "You don't understand how hard it is to be a journalist in Novolica. Against the Prelicans. You have no idea how many of us have been accused of mentirring and killed. It's not your lives on the line if I air this without some type of substantial proof. I'll be called in within a few hours and you'll never see me again. I've worked too long and too hard for it to end like this."

She had made her point. Roger nor Marela could think of a response. They all sat there silently.

Jolla stood up and walked over to the other side of the lounge area still holding her mug. She took a long sip and closed her eyes. She then turned and looked at a display showing an exotic view. She took a few deep breaths while eyeing the display.

Jolla slowly stepped back toward them holding her mug closely to her mouth, one arm being supported by the other.

"Maybe… if you had heard it yourself Maree… then maybe it would be different. But after what's been said about him—I cannot go on record with this."

Roger sighed. "What if you tell us exactly how you connect to the hub? I know the waves work differently for nationwide broadcasts. If you could show us how, you wouldn't need to risk anything."

Roger locked eyes with Jolla. She ignored him and looked back at Marela.

"He's right. That is all we need. Then we will be gone and … and you can watch our views skyrocket all over Novolica. Something this big will get a lot of attention."

Marela had struck a nerve. Jolla threw her mug on the table with a loud thud as it circled lightly around its bottom edges before steadying.

Marela is better at this. I better leave the convincing to her. Anything I say will probably sway her the other way. Roger looked at Marela from the corner of his eye. She sat perfectly still and calm.

"It would have to be you, Marela," said Jolla. "That is the only way we have a shot at this. There is simply no way I can air a firsthand account from him after what he has been accused of. I really don't think anyone will take him seriously."

Marela's smile faded.

"What exactly are you expecting me to do? Get on there and say I know all this to be true of my own accord?"

"Exactamente," responded Jolla.

"You are forgetting one critical thing. I work at the facility that builds the mentir detectors. I am under contract to not discuss anything I see or work on in that building. Not only would the content be against the rules to use—I would lose my assignment and be threatened with serious legal action if I am attached to the news at all."

Roger blinked rapidly. *I didn't think about that. Why hasn't she mentioned this before? I don't want her taking this kind of risk.*

He turned to her and started to speak. Marela held up a finger in front of him. Not once taking her gaze from Jolla. Roger eyed her longingly.

Jolla's eyes darted between the two of them, then she backed away from the rotating table and started pacing. Once she had turned away Marela looked at Roger sideways and smiled.

Hm, this is all part of her plan. It is her friend, after all. She knows her best.

Marela took out her handheld and started typing. She held up her device and waited for the slit that was located on the opposite side of the rotating table to come back around. When it reached them she forced her handheld into the slot. The table stopped quietly for a moment and then sank low into the floor. It lifted back up and revealed three new mugs in the compartment. Marela took two of them and walked to Jolla.

Jolla snapped out of her trance when Marela appeared right behind her, shoving the drink in her face.

"What's this?"

"This is to celebrate your work in exposing the Chancellor as a traitor and untrustworthy leader."

She moved the mug right under Jolla's nose. A wide smile crept upon her cheeks.

"Aww, my favorite. I haven't had Peachy Jum Jum in ages. I didn't even realize we had some here to be honest. This thing was stocked years ago."

"I knew you'd have some," replied Marela.

"The perfect drink for a celebration. We will have another one when that bastard is out of office." Jolla looked into her friend's eyes. She accepted the mug and clinked it against Marela's before they drank in unison.

Roger inhaled deeply. Picking up the third mug, he examined the orange liquid inside.

Peachy jum jum? What the hell is that?

He raised the mug to his nose and took a few short whiffs. He made a gagging noise. He took a small sip and it immediately glued his tongue to the roof of his mouth. He held his throat closed for a few seconds. Forcing his squinted eyes to open again, he looked up to see both Marela and Jolla snickering at him.

"Can't handle the PJ, huh?" commented Jolla.

"I don't blame him," added Marela. "He didn't grow up with this stuff like everyone in La Bajo does. I learned to appreciate the fruity goodness early in life."

The women raised their mugs again and drank heartily. Roger stared back into his mug. He forced himself to swallow first and tipped his mug up for a larger gulp once his throat had recontracted. Though it was chilled, he felt a hot burn in his throat as the liquid continued down into his stomach. He tried to wiggle his tongue around the inside of his mouth to rid himself of the taste.

Marela and Jolla had begun happily chatting about other topics. Roger's eyes started to glaze over as he watched them go back and forth. He found himself putting his mug back up to his mouth automatically. The drink went down much smoother this time. After some time, the strong urge to urinate came upon him. He stood up quietly.

"Ughh excuse me, Jolla," he said in the most polite tone he could muster given the urgency.

She looked over at him. Her expression this time was happy and much more obliging. She eagerly waited for what he was going to say.

"Umm, where is the bathroom down here? I need to step in for a minute."

She took another sip of her Peach Jum Jum and then set down her mug. She walked over to him and with a blushing expression she motioned for him to follow her down a corridor.

Once he turned on his heel, his balance shifted. He tried to steady himself as he followed. At the end of the hall, she turned back toward him. With a sly grin, she sized him up and down.

"Here it is," she said, motioning to a small chamber across from them. "I can show you how everything works if you want."

Her fingers had reached her hair and she was lightly stroking one side of it. Roger looked back behind them nervously.

"She can't hear or see us back here. Don't tell me you're still waiting for her after all this time. After what you have both been through. Not to mention everything she had with Briyano. That mess is going to stick with her forever. Why would you torture yourself like that? You know you have ... other options."

She caressed his arms slowly, looking deeply into his eyes.

What... what's going on?

Roger tried to step away from her, his legs now immovable cinder blocks weighted to the floor. His body turning to stone. Jolla took his silence for consent. Still gripping his arms tightly, she pulled him closer. Into her intimate space. She mushed his crotch into her abdomen. She stood up on the tips of her toes to reach his face, trailing her fingers around his ear.

"You know I can show you around in there if you aren't sure how to use everything. I don't mind lending a ... helping hand."

No no no, this isn't what I want. I have to resist this. I... it's Marela I want.

Her free hand slid down his chest. Gliding below his waistline.

This has to stop now!

Roger locked her wrist in an iron grip. Finally able to wrench himself sideways, freeing himself from her snare.

"Have you gone in yet? You're not the only one that has to go."

Marela was standing in the corridor only a few steps behind them.

Oh no! How long has she been there?

He lunged away, arms outstretched.

"This isn't what it looks like. Not saying it looks like anything. What does it look like to you?"

"What does what, look like? I need to go so are you going in or not?"

"You go ahead, I'll go in after you."

Marela walked past him, eying him skeptically. She and Jolla exchanged looks. Once the opening was shut behind Marela, Jolla faced him again, grinning.

Without any explanation, she brushed by him, leaving him in the corridor alone.

After Marela and Roger had both relieved themselves and returned to the lounge, the three of them discussed potential broadcasts about the Chancellor's treachery. Jolla was now addressing Roger directly and taking notes on his ideas for the plan.

"We will have to start local first," insisted Jolla. "That is the only way this will work. La Bajo is the perfect place since there are plenty of people who hate the Chancellor and will believe anything said against him."

"How do we know the story will go beyond that though?"

Marela leaned forward on the edge of her chair as she spoke.

"There is no guarantee someone from the other provinces will pick it up. Is it worth the risk? This could doom us from the start and then no one will know about it. Once it's dead, there's no coming back. It will be another rumor from our hometown."

They circled round and round on this topic.

"And we'll set it to air repeatedly before his evening addresses. It will be on everyone's mind as soon as they see the Chancellor. Even if they do not fully believe it, they will not be able to resist wondering. I'll make sure I personally deliver this to a few contacts I have that may push it further."

Marela was quiet.

"So it's settled then," Roger concluded. "We'll record the first snippet tomorrow and then start running the story twice a day on the Hub here in La Bajo for the next two weeks. Then we'll reevaluate to see if the story starts to pick up any momentum. If it does—"

"WHEN it does," added Jolla confidently.

"Right," Roger said, rolling his eyes continuing.

"The next step then is to record a new snippet and make the second version national."

"By then there will be more people paying attention and it will seem like you are giving more exclusive information," Marela finally chimed in.

"You nailed it. This is going to work and it will make me a famous hub broadcaster. People will seek me out from all over Novolica to air their stories, their desires, their passions. Jolla de la Soul Stanford will be known all over the world." She gazed out into the open air, wide-eyed in fantasy.

Marela checked the time. "It's getting late—we should head out somewhere for supper and then turn in."

"Well, you'll be staying here of course, Maree. We'll get the broadcast footage early so you can be on your way by noon."

"Am I to assume you are offering Roger a place to sleep as well?"

"Yes. Only—a few of the rooms are being redecorated and I've only kept up one of the guest areas. I'm sure the two of you won't mind sharing a bed for a night."

"That's fine. What's good to eat around here? I'm sure there are tons of new places that have popped up since I was last here."

"Well let me think. There's always Low Standards, they have really good fish. Or another one of my favorites, Bite-Sized. If you have a taste for authentic La Bajo classics, those are the places you want!"

We're sharing the same bed tonight. She agreed so casually. Jeez, I am starving though.

"Which one is closer?" Roger grabbed his stomach.

"Low Standards is right around the bend. Probably about a ten-minute walk on the passway. Unless you still have that wind bike of yours handy, Maree," she said with a snicker.

"We didn't want to bring it this far. They aren't as comfortable for long trips."

"Bummer, I remember when you first learned how to ride. You wouldn't stay off that thing—I mean, literally jumping on it for every little trip! I was looking forward to seeing it again after so much time."

"Maybe next time, J. Besides, if everything goes well with our first airing, we'll be back in no time to give you more content."

A small restaurant not far from Jolla's pod sat isolated. Low Standards was very small looking on the outside. The "L" and the "S" in the Low Standards sign were hanging loosely at risk of falling at any moment. There were broken patches of glass on the side end of the building. There was an unusual odor filling the space inside accompanying a large crowd.

"Not too shabby," said Marela as soon as they had entered the main slider.

Is she joking? I can't tell if she's being sarcastic.

Marela was smiling lightly, taking in the scene. Jolla on the other hand was looking around nervously, staring at each face in the room. She grabbed both Roger and Marela's arms and ushered them into a side corner of the space, where she placed the chairs around the table so she was blocked from being seen by others in the restaurant.

"What's going on here, J? Trying to stay out of sight… hiding from someone maybe?"

Trying to appear occupied with her handheld, Jolla repied nonchalantly, "No, I just know a lot of people that come here is all."

They swiped their handhelds across the transparent screen on the table between them, searching for food options.

"What is a spicy beretta?" Roger asked.

Before Marela could answer, Jolla excitedly turned into his local guide.

"It's like a chunk of meat that is filled with all kinds of things. Here they put beans, stew, and oranges in there. I'd vote to PASS."

Roger caught Marela rolling her eyes.

"How about a Mill Noche?"

"Oh yea those—" started Marela before immediately being cut off.

"Think of that like a platter of random items all spun up into one single dish that you can eat with your hands. It is SUPER filling and has a sample of meats, cheeses, veggies, and starches that will make you feel tired for days. The last time I had a Mill Noche here I slept in for three days straight. Even the leftovers lasted a whole week after."

"Yea those aren't bad," Marela chimed in finally with an air of defiance.

The three of them made their food choices and swiped their fingers forward to send the requests to the kitchen.

In no time, they were all stuffing their mouths with plates of La Bajo cuisine. Roger ordered the Mill Noche. Marela ordered something called a Chili Splicer which turned out to be a large piece of fish that looked like the lower half of a giant cockroach with a green substance oozing from its belly. Jolla ordered what she called her favorite La Bajan dish known as a Dirty Salad—a large bowl of legumes and starchy substances mixed with a bright red sauce and a thick white creamy sauce.

They smiled cheerfully as they both devoured every bit of their meals. After dinner they agreed on what their plan was moving forward. Roger would work on writing out an account of what he had overheard from the Chancellor and his staff member. Jolla would provide feedback on the story along the way. They wanted to make sure to maximize the effectiveness of everything he was saying. According to Jolla, each word, sentence and even the pauses between must be carefully planned and rehearsed. They wouldn't get a second chance to get this story out.

As they all turned in for the night, Roger began looking over the notes for his story on his handheld as he and Marela walked the corridor to their sleeping area. They had plenty of room to move about and a workspace for Roger to finish the speech. Marela went directly to the wash station.

"I am exhausted. I hope the washroom is stocked and ready."

As she entered the washroom, Roger sat down at the workspace to work on his speech.

Make it real, make it captivating. It has to make sense and the story has to flow. People need to hear this and fully understand.

He typed a few more words out. A light whoosh of air came from the other side of the room. Roger froze in place. He sat upright and scrunched his fingers together awkwardly. He turned around to see that the washroom had been left open. He could hear the shower water running.

He tried to keep his eyes on the document. His neck was straining not to move. Though somehow his chin forcibly pointed toward the washroom. There was steam starting to build. He couldn't quite see what his mind was wandering toward. He leaned back more and more. He subtly shifted his body at an angle.

Then the outline of her crept into view. Her skin, partially hidden but still glistening from the water and steam. Her curls now thoroughly soaked and splattered down the midpoint of her back. She was halfway facing away from him. Roger felt a dryness take over his mouth. He couldn't breathe, he could not even swallow. He tried to catch himself, mouth now gagged open. He could see her rotate toward him. He hurriedly turned around, hoping that she didn't catch him in the act.

The speech. Focus on the speech. What comes next?

He jotted a few things down that made absolutely no sense. His mind was still firmly situated on the washroom. He heard the funnel of water abruptly stop and his heart sank.

Dammit, she saw me. She won't be happy about this.

"ROG," he heard her calling out to him. He looked up and forced a large gulp down his throat.

"Hey, you need something?"

"Yes, can you come in here please?"

At the sound of these words Roger immediately wanted to jump to his feet and do as he was told.

Go. GO. Stand up now, toughen up. I— can't move.

He nudged his knees to knock the feeling back into them. They felt limp, nothing was moving. His limbs, reduced to spaghetti noodles. He could hear the loud thumping of his heart ringing in his ears.

"Sure—coming," he said after a long pause.

Ok. On the count of three I'll go in. One... two...

He heaved himself up from where he was sitting and tiptoed into the washroom to avoid being too eager. Steam still filled the area even though the water had stopped running. His nostrils filled with warm air. Once he had gotten closer to her his eyes widened. She was half turned toward him, standing there in the middle of the washroom completely soaked and free of any garments. She pointed to a high shelf.

"I can't reach the towels," she said softly.

He moved in closer to see where she was pointing to. The perfect outline of her naked body, now clearly visible to him. As he stepped in, her backside rubbed against him. He had spotted the pile of towels placed high up above the spigot for the washer. He gently placed one of his hands on her side to guide her out of the way, making room for him to grab the first towel.

He had broken his trance from her for a second. One long moment he dreaded. Once he finally turned back toward her, she was looking at him squarely. Her large round brown eyes, gazing back into his. He could see himself in the aura of her pupils. He reached his hand up slowly, brushing against her wrist and gliding up her arm. She leaned into him, wrapping her arms upward, clasping tightly around his neck.

They embraced, causing a warm burst of pure energy. Their lips touched. In the blink of an eye, they were passionately locked into one another, connected, and bound. Roger's mind was whisked away into bliss. The surrounding fixtures dissolved into thin air. The two remained tightly woven as her body pressed against his. His hands, tightly tied behind her back just above where her sloping posterior began. Days, hours, seconds ticked by—yet no time had passed at all. That night was the happiest and warmest Roger had felt in as long as he could remember. In bed they remained interlocked together until the sunlight.

CHAPTER SEVENTEEN

Grim Exposé

The next morning they went down the corridor to the main area of the pod together. Jolla was waiting and jumped to her feet once she spotted them.

"Let's get out there while we still have this beautiful lighting. And before we eat anything, you do not want to look bloated for this segment. Are you ready for the most important clip of your life?"

She smiled wide eyed at Roger. He smiled back.

"We are going to do what's right and expose the Chancellor for the charlatan he is," said Roger standing resolute.

"Ok, follow me then."

Jolla led them into a new area of the pod—a garage with three transportation models. Jolla's vehicles were pristine with fine finishes.

Wow, I wonder how much these cost.

She had two hover scooters sitting side by side. One was a bright pink color with light green trim around the edges. The second hover scooter looked to be the same model, only the panels to get inside had been removed and the color scheme had a more traditional storm gray look.

The third transport looked like a less expensive version of a power glider. Instead of the large spacious frame with the typical jet black finish, this one was small, and more compact. It was white with short bearings out to the side and rounded edges. The label on the side read "SKABLOO" Made In Tertisa. Marela read this and took a half a step backward.

"This is from Tertisa?" she asked, astounded. "Are you sure this thing is safe to operate?"

"Of course, Maree, relax. I've taken this out flying a load of times. They have to certify it here before you get the credentials to pilot it. So there's nothing to worry about. It's basically the same as a power glider, only cheaper."

Marela's apprehensive expression didn't change. Jolla used her handheld to open the garage and start the Skabloo's engine. The side panels opened upward in a butterfly wing motion.

Jolla went in first and sat down in the pilot seat. Roger and Marela followed and situated themselves in the two open seats to the right and behind her. Due to the small space in the back, Roger had to sit up front with Jolla. The inside of the Skabloo was very detailed. The controls in front of Jolla appeared intricate, yet simple to operate.

Ooh, this is actually comfortable, though the seats are small.

"How far away is this special backdrop for the video?" asked Marela.

She was forced to lean sideways, now resting her arms in the pockets ingrained deeply in the off-brand power glider's stitching. Jolla plugged her handheld into the main console. Using her finger she dragged what was showing on the tiny screen and expanded it over the top part of the glider. All three of them looked up at the floating, transparent diagram. There were two blinking dots on this map. One was a blinking triangle and represented where they were now. The other was a stable red dot marking their destination. At the bottom of the readout was an estimated time of arrival of 09:17.

"Great, we'll be there in no time. Let's get under way—it's cramped back here," said Marela.

Jolla pushed a bright yellow button on the console. They were instantly lifted off the floor of the garage. She grabbed the control sticks and leaned forward. The Skabloo took off, pushing them all to the backs of their seats as the garage closed behind them.

It climbed higher and higher into the sky and Jolla's pod quickly became an unrecognizable dot. There was not much traffic in the air, though they did have to maneuver around a few other vehicles. Bright green markers showed the different sky lanes.

The blinking blue triangle on the map above them moved closer to the destination. Roger scanned his handheld to review the speech he prepared the night before.

I never finished it. I got too distracted after Marela's shower. Last night was amazing. I wonder when we'll get to be alone again. I better write the rest out.

He began typing frantically. His stomach let out a loud growling noise.

"There's a great pub near the recording site for food. And they are fast, so don't worry about it," exclaimed Jolla.

Both Roger and Marela let out loud sighs of relief. Arriving at the location, Jolla leaned forward, twisting her arms side to side frantically trying to find a landing place. Once they were grounded, the side panels lifted upward to let them exit.

They were at the sight of a historic monument put in place before the Prelican regime took over Novolica. The monument was tall and wide. Its large side edges were filled with hand carved messages. The monument was shaped like a pod with people gathering on top of it.

"What exactly does this place mean to people from La Bajo?" asked Roger. Both Marela and Jolla were gazing at the creation with intense awe.

"This is where it all started for La Bajo," Jolla explained. "The people that governed us before the Restoration. Our ancestors have lived on this land for centuries. The people circling around the middle figure represent guardians. They protected us and provided a way of life where we could all trust each other. Some say the Prelicans ruined La Bajo and pushed us into the state we're in today. We have the lowest

successful placement rates and the most unhappy people in all of Novolica. La Bajans have been wanting change for years now. That's why this
is where we're getting the footage. You see all those names inscribed on
the sides? La Bajans come here to write the names of loved ones they've
lost to failed mentir screenings. Here people can express their outrages,
concerns, and hardships as a result of the Prelican regime without fear
of being called in. Now we'll use this publicly as our beacon of hope."

A concerned look came across Roger's face.

"What's wrong, having second thoughts?" Marela said sarcastically.

He tried to force a smile. "No, it's just that I'm not actually from La
Bajo. Will it do more harm than good that it'll be MY face, showing
in front of this place?"

"Don't worry about that," replied Jolla. "Since we are only placing
this on the La Bajo hub channels for now, no one will even think twice
about it. They will know it was made by and for them within our city.
Let's do it now."

Jolla opened the rear compartment of the SKABLOO and pulled
out two lighting poles and an extra large handheld device. Roger and
Marela helped her carry the equipment to the front of the statue. She
pointed the light poles to a central area and positioned them out of
view of the oversized handheld she was now framing. Roger looked at
his device and read over the material a few times.

"I don't think I'll be able to memorize all of this. Is there a way I can
do it and have the lines too?"

"Sure, I'll be standing close enough that any words on my hub
handheld should be visible to you. Send me the text."

Roger made a few taps on his personal device and swiped upward
toward Jolla's hub device. Within a few moments, his words had appeared in floating, dark large print above the large handheld clearly
enough for him to read. He stood in place between the two light poles.
After a big deep breath, he recited the words that were now moving
slowly in front of him. Marela was standing adjacent to Jolla, focusing
on every word he was saying.

"My name is Roger Allen Aimes, your candidate for Chancellor of Novolica. You've been led to believe that our current Chancellor is an honorable man who lives by the rules that have governed our society since the Restoration War. I've now learned through my time as a candidate that this is false. Before our last event, as I was waiting in the prep rooms to be screened, I heard the Chancellor himself speaking. He revealed that the mentir jigs used by himself and the Prelican elites prevent them from being found guilty of mentirring. Yes, as long as the Chancellor is using his personal X5 jig, he cannot be harmed. They've been the biggest offenders of a crime we've all suffered from, via friends, loved ones, or coworkers. This entire time, the system and the rules that are supposed to keep us safe and govern us, only apply to us. If some people are allowed to be exempt from mentir screening, no one should have to suffer another inquiry.

"Do you want to know what the Chancellor really thinks about us? I'll tell you. When it was determined that he and I would have to use the same mentir detector, he was disgusted. He hated the idea that I would be saved and reap the benefits of using his X5, knowing that neither of us would have a chance to be killed. To prevent any suspicion from changing the machines, he was forced to go along with it. He would have much rather had me and all of you risk our lives every time we are called in. Yet, he exempts himself.

"The leader of our nation is supposed to be the most honest of all. Now we have the complete opposite. Now is our time to stand up and get rid of this system that has torn our families apart and made us fear connections with new people. Together, we will banish mentir screenings for good. Support me as your new Chancellor and have a real chance at living a long and prosperous life."

Though the words were shown in front of him to read, he still stumbled during certain parts. He ran out of breath at times, and other times he insisted on starting over. Finally after seven takes, all three of them had agreed there was enough content to make a compelling story.

"There'll be more editing than I would have hoped for, but I think the final version will be great! Well done, Roger!"

Once all of the equipment they used to create the recordings had been stored away, they tucked into the SKABLOO again and took off for breakfast.

GREEN STIX read the sign across the front of the restaurant. Inside the ceilings were tall, intricate designs. Elaborate artwork of different shapes and sizes filled the walls. Even the floor was painted different colors in distinct areas of the pub. There were only a few people present. Jolla led them to a set table area near a few large silver framed shutters and sat herself down. She pulled out her handheld to see the menu options. Roger and Marela did the same.

"Where is everyone?" Marela said aloud. "I would think a place like this would be completely full at this time."

Jolla looked at her puzzled but didn't answer. Marela scoffed.

After eating, Jolla promised she would have the recording ready in two days.

"Maree, I'll send it to you directly. Once you get back to Finca, you won't be able to find it on your hub channels. And don't worry, I'll keep you posted on the response from everyone around here."

~

A week had passed since Roger and Marela returned from La Bajo. There had been no communication with Jolla who was not answering any calls or messages from Marela. Roger figured she was probably still editing the footage. Marela was becoming increasingly anxious about it, though. When they were home she flipped rapidly through all of the hub channels expecting to hear news of Roger's story that had spread outside of La Bajo.

Roger tried his best to calm her down. Nothing worked. Despite this, every night since they had gotten back from La Bajo, Marela would come into his room to sleep with him. This made Roger feel invincible. Like nothing else in the world mattered. It made his motivation to help change Novolica stronger than ever.

After nine days of waiting, Marela's handheld buzzed showing a hub recording of Roger in La Bajo discussing everything he had overheard.

"It looks amazing! Jolla was able to clean up all of my mess ups."

"Yea, I agree this final version looks impeccable. I'd better call her and apologize for all of the nasty messages I left over the past few days."

According to Jolla, she had already posted the playback on the hub channels in La Bajo using her work credentials. She assured them that as soon as she heard anything, she would let them know.

"The approval ratings are still open, right?" asked Roger.

"I mean when people see this and the word starts spreading, there's a chance that another event could be scheduled. Maybe we should check over the guidelines again."

"Yes, people can still add to your approval rating even though right now you do not have the score to continue."

"Once word gets out about the bogus mentir screenings, the news will be everywhere. People will be angry and demanding you come back to take the Chancellor's place."

She seems so confident. I know we can do this together.

"People know that you are connected to me," Roger replied after a period of silence. "Things may get interesting over the next few weeks. Once my story is spread past La Bajo, everyone in Novolica will want to know what's going on and will want answers. I suspect the Prelicans won't be happy about this."

He spoke deliberately to lead up to the final point he wanted to make.

"Marela, I don't think it's safe for you to keep going to work."

He held his breath waiting for her to respond. She looked back at him.

"Well, I have considered the idea that the Chancellor and his people may respond hostilely to us leaking this information. I tried to reassure myself knowing that we are doing the right thing. Not to mention we have a load of people out there supporting you. But… I think you are right. Until the next event is scheduled we will have to be cautious. I'll stay away from work and I also think we should live somewhere else temporarily. Make it harder to find us in case there is any danger waiting."

"Whoa, wait a minute. I didn't say anything about leaving our pod. With both of us not working, I don't think we can afford somewhere new. There's no way the Prelicans would be so brazen as to attack us in our home, right? Everyone would know about it, and they would be finished."

"I'm not so sure anyone would know. Think about it. They have been able to get away with evading mentir machines for how long now? There have always been rumors of people who oppose them disappearing unexpectedly. We have to assume anything is possible."

"It makes sense I guess."

"Well we have to wait until the approval rating goes up first. Otherwise, none of it will matter anyway."

Marela bit down on her bottom lip, contemplating everything.

"I guess we stay here for now until we get a new development."

A few days had passed and after checking the pre-existing approval results on their handhelds every day. Roger's rating did start to increase. He went from two points to three, then four. Jolla informed him that the recording had been picked up by a small hub channel in Leiton City. That same night, his rating jumped to eight points. It was only a matter of time until he could challenge the Chancellor again publicly. Once the Leiton City hub channel started airing what Roger had said, his rating increased daily.

"You are getting close," yelled Jolla over their live feed.

She had been calling Marela twice a day now to report all of the activity happening in La Bajo. People were furious there and the majority of the citizens fully believed what Roger had shared and resolved to forcibly remove the Chancellor if needed. So far, no public statements had been made about the video that was now circulating on many of the most watched hub channels.

Nine days had passed since Jolla first released the final cut in La Bajo. Roger's rating was now at sixteen percent. It was only a matter of time for him to reach twenty percent to officially become a candidate again. That afternoon, he received a call from a familiar voice.

"Mr. Aimes, Stacey Worchester here—I sincerely hope you remember me."

His voice sounded shaky and not nearly as distinct as it had been in person.

"With everything going on around your—uh, recent statements—it's been decided that another event is needed."

Stacey continued on in a hurried fashion. "We will need to create footage of you accepting your bid to candidacy once again as we expect you'll be reaching the twenty percent requirement. Therefore, please come tomorrow morning to the Renaissance building alone by 09:00. Well, see you then. Good day."

Before Roger could confirm his attendance or ask any questions, Stacey ended the call. A grin spread across Roger's face.

It's happening.

He rushed into the main part of the pod to tell Marela about the good news.

"Why such short notice? They didn't mention what you should bring? Will it be open with an audience like the other events? Why have they not disclosed more details?"

"Obviously they aren't happy about all of this. The Prelicans are being exposed and now they are forced to acknowledge me and restart the process. His superiors are probably furious. This is something they have never had to do. It's the only explanation."

Marela looked worried. "I'm not sure, it seems—off. Though I guess the only thing there is to do is go."

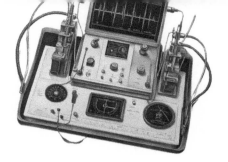

CHAPTER EIGHTEEN

Bloody Escape

After a restless night with little sleep, Roger woke up early the next day to get to the Renaissance building. Although nervous, he was eager to accept his new bid as a candidate. He was careful not to wake Marela.

Today we take a big step to get the Chancellor out of office.

He headed out of the pod and to the shiloh station.

Commuters filled every corner of the shiloh, bunching in whatever small space they could occupy. At the next stop, some people shuffled in and out of the compartment. Roger's body tensed. He turned around slowly, but the eyes he thought were staring at him had moved. The hairs on the back of his neck stood up.

I could've sworn there was someone watching me just now. Something doesn't feel right.

He moved over to let a few people pass. Turning back to the spot where the eyes once were, another figure shifted out of view. Buried amongst the other passengers. There was a crowd of people standing near him. Most were occupied with their handhelds.

It's ok, just breathe. The stop is coming up.

As the shiloh approached Leiton City, Roger moved quickly toward the exit. He glanced behind him but couldn't make out the mysterious figure he lost sight of earlier.

A loud BUZZ rang and the sliders from each compartment opened. He hurriedly walked out into the station. The crowd closed in around him with people entering and leaving.

Five men dressed in dark clothes were moving toward the shiloh, aggressively pushing people out of their way. Roger shuffled along with the crowd toward the station exit. The men were now halfway between Roger and the exit slider.

They look like trouble.

Roger tried to move laterally away from their path. A hard nudge pushed him forward. He stumbled into someone else to catch his balance. Steadying himself, he turned around to see who had shoved him. There was a loud whale sounding noise followed by the power suddenly being cut. It was pitch black. Roger couldn't see a thing.

"What was that?'"

"What's going on?"

"HEY! What happened to the lights?"

"The sliders aren't opening!"

People started yelling. Roger felt around to avoid bumping into any-one but people were now moving swiftly around him in all directions. He felt a hand on his shoulder, and at least two sets of hands grabbing one of his outstretched arms. There was a large crack against the side of his head. Then—nothing. Complete darkness.

A rattling noise hummed in the distance. His head felt heavy and his body was contorted awkwardly. Roger tried opening his eyes and only saw the cover on his face. Now lying down with his limbs bound tightly together, the only movement he could manage was rocking sideways, trying to maneuver off his blindfold. His left eye was free.

What the hell happened? I can't move. I can hear an engine. This... this looks like a power glider.

The signature pointed design around the edges was visible from the inside. Roger began to panic.

I've been taken. I've got to get out of here!

He wiggled around, turning his body sideways. The blindfold fell to his cheekbones.

A partition separated him from the main cabin. He leaned against it.

The engine is running, they must be coming back soon!

His heart pounded. Leaning against the partition he pushed hard with his shoulder. Then bumped it with the side of his ear. Now he was banging against it repeatedly trying to force his body through. He lifted his elbows as high as he could while tied up. With all the concentrated force he could muster, he smashed right through the divider.

A loud BASHING noise rang through the power glider. He had no time to wait, no time to think if anyone heard or saw the glass break. Instinctively he rolled over the glass shards toward the front, slashing his side and chest open and ripping through his clothes. He crawled to the pilot seat, blood leaking down his front, hands and legs still bound together by a metallic wiring coiled tightly around his wrists and ankles.

He banged his knee on the console to the right of the pilot seat as he wriggled into the chair. Roger struggled to sit himself upright while still bound.

I've never driven a power glider before. Jolla! It looks like the Skabloo.

He mimicked what he had seen Jolla do and pulled back on the lever with both hands since they were still lashed together. Then he grabbed the two control sticks in front of him and pushed forward. Nothing happened.

Someone began yelling outside. Three large individuals were running toward the power glider. He looked down quickly to find an activator of some sort. Time was running out. The men were getting nearer. One of them pulled a weapon from his side. As he pointed it toward the power glider, Roger felt his feet brush against a pedal. He pushed down on it hard and the glider zipped forward.

In an instant he was hovering faster than he could react. He tried turning the joysticks left and right, jerking them hard as struggled to control the machine. He narrowly missed bumping a nearby passway.

He leaned backward hard, pulling the controller with him. The power glider zipped off into the sky, throwing him backward into the seat.

In the air, he had to lean his whole body into every maneuver due to his binds.

What the hell just happened!

Where were they taking me? If I hadn't escaped, what would have happened?

Roger tried to force deep breaths, inhaling through his nostrils.

Prelicans.

They must be trying to stop me from re-declaring as a candidate. But how did they know where I was?

Roger clenched his jaws together.

Dammit—my handheld! They must have my signal tracked.

Roger felt for the device in his slitted pocket. With hands tied together he struggled to search without losing control of the power glider. Though his clothing was tattered, the pocket was intact. Yet, the handheld was gone.

I'm alone. I'm hurt bad. Stranded in the middle of who knows where. No communication.

Roger's body trembled. Blood continued to flow from the cuts across his torso.

The glider—they'll probably track me with this. Like Marela can find her windbike, they must know exactly where I am and where I'm headed.

I'm not getting caught again. There's no telling what will happen to me if the Prelicans find me.

Roger felt around the pilot console and pressed the button behind the shift lever. A floating menu display appeared. There was a map option, showing him where he was.

Looks like I'm still in Leiton City but on the outskirts. Where can I go? I need to get rid of this power glider as soon as possible. I don't want to be anywhere near this city. How will I travel out of sight? All of the shiloh stations are filled with ID sensors. They'd find me in minutes. I'll have to travel on something they can't track. Think—think dammit!

I... I need a windbike. No, they can't go that far and you can spot them easily. Maybe something on land would be better. If not a street traveler, it'd have to be a rover. That will help me travel fast on land. Where in the hell can I find a rover? Who was that guy Charly told me about that one time? His relative that owned a recreational vehicle shop. Some guy who rejected his assignment and got involved with illegal dealings after starting his own business.

Roger was sure that this guy would have no problem bargaining a brand new fully loaded power glider for a cheap terrain rover.

What was his name? Think... Let me think...

Jonathan... Jonas... Jason?

It has to be a "J" something. I remember because the name reminded me of my own cousin Jackson.

Jester...

No Joston...

He thought hard again about the name of the shop itself.

JETSON'S JETTISONS.

That's right! Charly was commenting on how the shop name had nothing to do with vehicles but because his name was Jetson, he wanted to make it sound appealing.

Roger keyed in Jetson's Jettisons on the large floating map display and a target dot appeared in an outpost town about an hour away. Following the path now outlined with blinking chevron symbols, he maneuvered the power glider onto the course and pushed the pedal and lever as far forward as he could to reach maximum speed.

He couldn't settle himself. His breathing was raspy. Both legs were sweating profusely and feeling cramped due to the binds. Welts were now forming around his wrists from the metallic ties.

Trembling, he was on the verge of passing out at any moment from anxiety and blood loss. He constantly checked his surroundings for any sight of someone chasing him.

Finally when it was time to descend, he felt his body shake even more.

What if the Prelicans were able to remotely access the power glider's log files and see where I'm going? They could be waiting for me, already surrounding the shop.

His skin was cold and clammy. As the store came into view he circled around to park the power glider on the nearby passway.

Clothes tattered and drenched in blood, Roger scooted sideways out of the power glider and onto the lot. He bounced awkwardly from side to side attempting to hold his balance steady. Afraid to look left or right at who might be witnessing a bloodied man exiting a high-end power glider, he hobbled faster toward the shop entrance.

Then, his foot got snagged on an uneven piece of ground.

SKIIIR-BAAAMM

He landed solidly on the hard concrete, rattling his chin and face bones. There was red goo trickling all over the pavement from both his existing wound in his side and the new fresh cut now opened up over his mouth. He doubled over and scrunched his body in a crouching position struggling to move forward like an inchworm slinking across the earth.

Again he tried to steady himself and hoist back up to his feet without being able to spread his legs or arms apart. One of his eyes was swelling and the ground was starting to look fuzzy. He looked upward toward the direction of the shop to see how much further he had to go.

He saw a figure walking toward him. It was a man with a thick, full length beard. He was unnaturally thin. The man casually approached Roger, smiling at him.

"Hey fella, you alright there?"

Roger tried picking up his head higher.

"Well, I'll be damned," said the man again with a smirk.

"You're Roger Aimes, the challenger himself. What the hell happened to you?" The man leaned over to help Roger to his feet. As he was picking him up, Roger noticed he was wearing a buttoned custom shirt that read "JETSON" on one side and was labeled JETSON'S JETTISONS on the sleeve.

"Let's get you inside, bud."

He hoisted an arm under Roger's armpit and supported him toward the shop.

"Wait," Roger tried speaking through his swelling face. "I bus athacked by de Prelicans. Dey might be thacking de glider".

Jetson stared closely at Roger and then looked back at the power glider behind him.

"Don't you worry, I'll take care of it."

He moved faster now, dragging Roger's weight toward the building. Roger felt drowsy. As if he could pass out at any time. He tried to help Jetson support his weight as much as he could but started slipping in and out of conscience.

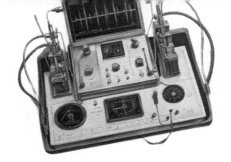

CHAPTER NINETEEN

This Never Happened

Roger opened his eyes weakly. He was lying on a large sofa with bandages wrapped around his midsection. His binds around his hands and legs had been removed. His head throbbed. There was medical tape across his chin and cheek bone.

He looked around, examining the strange place. The room was small with gray walls and an office credenza facing him. No windows or decorations anywhere. Only lit by a single light bulb sitting in the corner, barely visible. The slider to the room was on his left and had been heavily reinforced.

Why would anyone want to come in here? That slider looks unbreakable.

Roger sat up and looked behind him. There was a huge refrigerator that perfectly blended in with the walls.

Ahh, the power glider. I need to make sure they can't track me. Where's Jetson?

He forced himself to his feet and walked to the bolted slider. He heard a loud whizzing noise from behind him.

Is that coming from the refrigerator? I've never heard a fridge make that sound.

The whizzing grew louder and louder. The front compartment of the refrigerator opened on its own. Roger hobbled backward with his back now against the slider.

"What the hell?"

Out of the refrigerator walked the man that had picked him up off the passway. There was a bright light behind him that lit up the entire room. He hastily closed the compartment behind himself.

"I thought you'd still be passed out, friend. I was hoping I'd be sitting here, waiting for you to open those pretty, daring eyes of yours. We couldn't waste any time disabling the electronics on that glider you rode in here on. Wasn't too hard to figure out who tied you up and owned that glider. Still though, I want to hear it from you. And most importantly, I want to know how the hell you knew to come here... even though the answer to that might get you killed anyway."

Roger shuddered, leaning hard against the locked slider.

I'm trapped here. He helped me, now he's threatening to kill me. While complimenting my eyes, I think, in some secret room with a refrigerator exit.

Jetson stepped past the sofa and over to the credenza. He shuffled some things around under it and swiped his hand across it. This brightened the lights in the room.

"Relax, you're fine for now. Come sit down. I'm Jetson." He pointed two fingers to the sofa indicating to Roger to sit. Roger relented and hobbled over to the sofa.

"I'm Roger," he said while wincing, holding his bandaged side. "This all started—"

"How the hell do you know who I am?" Jetson cut in. His casual tone turned aggressive. He looked deranged with a menacing expression etched onto his face.

"Charly, your cousin. I work with him at the mine rows. He told us about you once, how you rejected the idea of being assigned a career and went off on your own. Charly is—one of my best mates. When I found myself in the Prelicans' stolen power glider, I was hoping I could trade it to you for a rover to get as far away from them as possible without being tracked."

Jetson's tough demeanor had changed back to the friendly, playful voice. He leaned back in his chair and put his feet up.

"Well, I'll be. My big-mouthed cousin, sending me gifts from far and wide. Don't worry about the glider, I took care of it already. That's what I was doing down in the cell you did not see me walking in from a few minutes ago."

Jetson had put a strong emphasis on "did not" and Roger understood the message.

"Seeing you all tied up and falling out of that new top-grade glider, I knew something was up. I've heard your story so I know you don't have the plinkos for a glider of that caliber. As soon as I got you inside, I went right out there and dragged that thing in here to strip it down. It's completely barren now. Won't be transmitting a goddamn thing to no one but me when I resell it at high margin."

"So in that case, you do have a land rover you can give to me?"

"Oddly enough my beaten down friend, I don't GIVE away anything."

"But you just said the glider is valuable. I'm the one that brought it in."

Jetson looked at him for a moment. His expression looked conflicted between indifference and outright pity for the man sitting in front of him.

"Not saying that I'll be giving you anything, but what exactly did you have in mind?"

Roger paused.

"I need something that will hold a charge for a few days. I can't let those Prelicans get hold of me again. I'm going off the grid. If you have something—anything that can get me to a far away outpost—the glider is yours."

Jetson chuckled as he stroked his beard.

"I hate those damn Prelicans. Lost my brother to a bullshit screening four years ago. As soon as I saw you were going up against that mentirring backstabbing asshole Prumpt, I added to your rating. I can see why they want to do you in. After that video you created, I guessed it would only be a matter of time until they got to you. You must have known they weren't going to let you walk in and jeopardize what they've been building for the last 40 years."

How could I have been so stupid? Of course trying something like this could get me killed.

Roger sunk low into the chair, burying his face in his hands.

"But, lucky for you, you found your way to me. I'll get you what you need. As long as you give me your word you'll come out on top and end these mentir screenings for good."

Roger looked up at him and nodded slowly.

"Ok then," said Jetson standing to his feet.

He pulled out his handheld and pointed it toward the slider. There was a loud CLINKING noise as it started to rotate outward.

"Follow me."

He led Roger out into the meticulously maintained shop. Every vehicle was categorized. He had windbikes, street travelers, gliders, and rovers. Once they arrived at the middle of the warehouse, he indicated for Roger to have a seat. Jetson disappeared to another part of the shop.

After some time, Roger began pacing. He limped awkwardly, covering his bandages. Finally Jetson reappeared gripping an unusually thick handheld in his left hand.

"Damn son, it's only been an hour. Man you are jittery. Guess I can't blame you after what happened. Anyway, I wanted to make sure what I'm about to give you was all charged up. Come see this."

He led him toward a large brown vehicle in the corner of the room. It had an angular shape with sharp edges. There were no windows on the land rover. Six large tires with deep ridges supported it.

"Now don't get too carried away. This is the best land rover I have. I'm expecting you to bring this back to me once the heat is off you. Better yet, once you become Chancellor, bring it back and provide funding for a new one on account of the loan interest. This one will probably be beat to shit once you finish with it anyway. Let's take a closer look."

He pointed the thicker handheld toward the machine. An opening appeared directly in front of them. A hatch lowered down, revealing the spacious interior.

The large control center had three pedals at the feet, two palm gripping levers and two control sticks at eye level. The pilot chair was thick and wide. Behind the control center was food, water, and supplies to last him for months. There were also blankets and a pillow in the back.

"Yeap, you say you want to go off the grid. This is what you'll need."

Jetson passed Roger the large handheld.

"This was built specifically for this rover. All of the controls, access, and directional functions are programmed on it. Without this, you can't operate the rover. I also put a burner handheld in there for you. There's some plinkos on it if you get jammed up."

Roger tucked the device under his arm.

"Now there's no time to waste. I'm sure you want to test it out, but it's been a few hours since you landed here. I'm sure the Prelicans will come up with some other way to track you. They'll never find that power glider, I've made sure of that. If they only find me here, they've wasted a trip. But if they find me and you here, we're done for."

"Ok, I'm outta here," Roger said as he moved to the pilot seat. He docked the handheld on the control center as Jetson left the rover.

Once the vehicle entrance to the showroom opened, he powered on the land rover and took off into the nearby underbrush. The body of the land rover matched the color of the terrain.

This is how I'll stay alive.

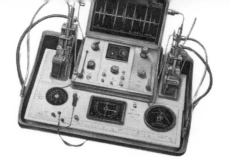

CHAPTER TWENTY

New Look Who Dis

Day three on the run. Roger crossed a thicket of trees amidst a wayward plain. He was the only living being in any direction for kilometers, cut off from the outside world.

I'll need to pull in somewhere and recharge.

He leaned back the pilot seat. It was 11:00 and the sun was bright.

How long until things are safe again? News of my absence must have spread. He removed the handheld device from the console and put it in front of his face. He looked worn out.

I can't go back. Going back would put her in danger. No doubt they have her under close watch. If I don't contact her, she'll be fine.

He repeated this to himself over and over again.

I need to hide out somewhere. No one can recognize me. I'll have to get altered. He opened the map on the handheld and did a search for **Trait Alteration Stations**. A few dots appeared on the map floating above him with the closest one being three days away if he continued to travel off the grid.

He selected the course that would take him through more jungle and marsh. He took a bite out of a dry meal he recently unpacked. After a few deep breaths, he leaned the seat upright and proceeded to push the land rover forward. He pitched awkwardly side to side as the vehicle passed over dense shrubs and fallen trees. Occasionally glancing up to see if there were any gliders flying above.

It had been hours since he last saw one. It was in the morning when the sun was still high. Now in the evening, there was no way he could be spotted from above, even if the land rover's cloaking mechanism wasn't activated.

The dark shade of brown it had been when Jetson gave it to him had now turned shrub green. It blended in perfectly with the area. If someone came closer, Roger could activate the full camouflage mode, coating the outside of the rover with the replicated look of its surroundings.

He continued on for another three days, stopping every few hours to rest in denser areas. He ate while he maneuvered the machine. The paranoia of being tied up lingered in his mind. He felt the bindings wrapped around his hands and feet whenever he thought about going outside the rover for air.

The map points here. Looks like the Trait Alteration Shop is just over the ridge. I'll leave the rover hidden here in the trees. I'll use a blanket to cover my face.

Roger's pace was brisk and he had already started to sweat with the blanket on his head.

This has to be it.

BUILD-A-BODY

OPERATING HOURS 08:00 - 18:30 7 days a week.

Roger pushed a button on the side of the wall that activated the slider and moved in quickly. Inside, there was a woman sitting in front of a row of compartments. Her hair was a bright turquoise. It had been cut short on one side with the other sticking up in the air and curved over. She had fiery red pupils that accentuated her slim, triangular jaw line. As she stood up to greet him, her body looked unnaturally perfect in shape and size. Roger reached instinctively for the tucked end of the blanket around his face.

"Don't worry about it," the woman stopped him. "We get plenty of people in here with scars, disfigurements, and the like. No need to remove the cover. We can still make the changes you want."

She motioned for Roger to come closer as she pulled out an electronic console and sat it on the counter in front of them. He looked at the catalog.

FACE
BODY
HAIR
VOICE
PERFORMANCE

"Since you don't have an appointment and we are near closing time, any voice or performance enhancements will need to be scheduled at a later date. Lucky for you, there isn't anyone else scheduled to come in today so all other enhancements can still be done. We're running a 3-for-1 special so if you decide to change hair length for example, we'll throw in one face or body alteration for no additional charge. As long as it's cosmetic and not structural we could knock it out in no time."

After making his selections from the list, a large bright light emitted from the device.

"Excellent! For the demo, you can enter the private dressing room in the back."

Roger picked up the device and headed to the private area. Once inside, he removed the blanket wrapped around his head. He lifted the console directly in front of him so that his face was now illuminated by the light emitting from the device.

The scanner traced his face and then turned off. After a few seconds, Roger was looking at his face being re-created both on the device and on the mirror in front of him. As he toggled through the various attribute changes, he could see what he would look like once they were completed.

He settled on thick blonde hair. It would be matted and fall over his face to hide his features. As an extra precaution, he added a long beard to make him even more unrecognizable.

Next he changed his eye color to hazel. On the large display, he added everything to the cart. Once the selections moved, the floating images on the device and mirror disappeared and he looked like his normal self once more. He replaced the covering over his head and went back to the main lobby.

She looked over what he had chosen and smiled back at him chuckling, "Not going for a more attractive look I see."

Roger wasn't amused by this comment and proceeded to pay. They moved to a back room where the shop owner motioned for him to sit down. The chair was cold and hard. Roger's legs were now suspended and his head tilted backwards. Above him was a large round dome connected to a monitor behind him he couldn't see.

"You ready?"

"Yes, let's do it."

He waited until the very last moment to remove his head covering. The store owner made a few taps on the monitor and the large dome moved over top of Roger's head. He felt a hot sensation surrounding his face as darkness filled his eyes.

"Ahh, it itches!"

"Stay still, it's almost over."

My skull is on fire! It's like my face is being split in half and my skin is going to melt.

Roger's body twisted and turned.

After a few seconds, the sensation was gone. Roger's vision had been restored and the dome was no longer on his face. The worker was smiling in front of him. Roger touched his head. He felt the thick and matted strands of hair now hanging down, covering his shoulders.

The long twisted blonde beard he'd chosen now hung from his invisible chin. He looked at the mirror and was shocked. The store owner sniggered hard under her breath after seeing Roger's reaction.

"Everything looks exactly like you selected. Your appearance will remain this way until you get re-altered at another certified station to return to normal."

"Thanks for all your help. Do you have a hair tie or something?"

She went to the alteration room and came back with a thick black band. He grabbed large bunches of the chunky twists and struggled to maneuver them into the band. Once they had finally been tied back, he focused again on the mirror now fully showing bright hazel eyes, once hidden by his hair ropes. Being satisfied with the new disguise, he thanked the lady again for helping him before leaving.

Back in the land rover, he pondered his options.

Eventually, I'll run out of plinkos. Then things will get more difficult. In disguise, I have more freedom.

"Marela," he sighed. "I have to find a way to contact her. She needs to know I'm ok."

He opened the land rover guidance map.

Going back to Finca isn't an option. I'm not going anywhere near the Prelican stronghold Leiton City. They'll probably be looking for me in La Bajo too because of the video.

He picked an outpost town. Right now he was in OL-IV west of Leiton City about 800 km from the city center. If he headed north he would have to cross through SI-XX which was mostly mining land and sparsely populated. If he headed south he would eventually arrive at JX-VII which he knew of for being a technology driven outpost where a lot of manufacturing took place for the entire nation. It was a three-day trip.

He selected a plot on the map located within JX-VII and maneuvered the land rover onto the outlined path.

The passways in the outpost town were filled with citizens. A brightly lit yellow and white sign read *Suenos Cumplidos Inn* in elegantly curved lettering. From outside, it looked very quiet with very few vehicles around the building. The main slider made a loud dinging noise as he entered.

At the check-in counter, the greeter bowed to Roger. "Welcome to the Suenos Cumplidos Inn, may I have a name for your reservation sir?"

Roger paused. "I'd like to register under a different name than my own."

"Of course Sir, we have many unregistered guests here. You won't be getting any inquiry submissions from me, I can assure you. I'll log you as #98 and tag your name as a decline to answer."

"Thank you. I'm not sure how long I'll be staying, what is the rate for an undefined stay?"

"Of course, Sir. We would require a sum of eight plinkos now and then five plinkos per week until the end of your stay."

That means one week of plinkos until I run out of money.

"Alright," Roger responded.

After he transferred payment, the attendant directed him to his pod. It was surprisingly cozy. The washroom was about the same size as the one in the pod he and Marela shared. The sitting area was also bigger than what he was used to and much more comfortable. There were ornate decorations providing a sense of relaxation.

Roger laid down his things and immediately went into the washroom. After a wash, he searched for work to earn plinkos. He was able to identify three potentials that did not require career replacements in the area.

I'll wake up early tomorrow before the first shifts start and ask for a position. He tucked himself in bed for the first time in a week and instantly passed out.

Roger was woken by the bright morning light shining through the glass shield in the front of his pod. He couldn't remember the last time he had slept so deeply.

"Damn, it's already so sunny."

He quickly turned over to look at the time on the land rover handheld sitting on the stand beside the bed. 10:00.

"SHIT!"

He threw himself sideways frantically, and darted around the area to find his clothes. His twisted hair swung wildly as he readied himself. He ran out and searched the way to the first location.

"Tor–Tu-Ga, interesting name."

He hustled on foot along the nearest passway entrance. He grossly underestimated the walking distance. By the time he arrived in front of a large metallic dome titled TORTUGA FACTORY, he was dripping with sweat and had a sharp stitch in his side. There was no one to be found in the front area, though he could hear the loud noise of heavy machinery coming from a distance.

He moved through the dome shaped building. All around him were metallic looking figurines. Some were shaped like animals and others like stick figures of people. Up against the walls were large bunches of metals wired together. He spotted someone on the other end of the room. They were pulling long pointed levers attached to a steel frame. Roger moved toward the neon-clad employee and tried to make himself as visible as possible. When she spotted him standing there she jumped backward a half step, startled.

"What… what can I do for you sir?" she said shakily over the noise of the machinery.

"I'm looking for a position here. I—uh recently decided to move away from my designated career for something new that I can start really soon. I could even start today. Just need to start making a few plinkos."

The employee was much more relaxed now and moved toward him with an outstretched hand. Her hair was braided in short bunches with a smile as wide as a river.

"I'm Robia," she said, shaking hands with Roger.

"I'm one of the foremen here. We have an open quorum in about two hours to discuss taking on new people. The process is pretty simple and with your height and build, I'm sure we'll have no problem with you joining the team. Come back then and go through that side wall with the new candidates."

Robia smiled and returned to operating the levers.

"Things are in motion," Roger said to himself.

He returned to Tortuga twenty minutes prior to the start of the open quorum. He made sure to enter the dome through the slider Robia had directed him toward. There were only nine people inside waiting including him. They all sat down in the dark blue tinted room. Each chair was shaped like an individual workspace with displays built into the armrests. Robia and two other workers stood in front and addressed everyone.

"Thank you all for coming today," Robia began. "We need additional workers as our placement levels have been too low to sustain production over the past three years. Here we produce alloys that are used to build sustainability all over Novolica.

"We're one of the last factories of its kind that uses people in every step of the process. Right now we are looking for more people to work the cast machines. Therefore, you'll need to be sufficiently strong. We anticipate two weeks of fully paid training and after that you'll be prepared to help us keep operations moving."

All nine job seekers nodded in agreement. One of the people standing next to Robia moved forward. He was a burly looking male in his late fifties.

"One more thing. We are looking for people to start as early as today depending on your previous experience. Since we are very short-handed, we're willing to take you all on to meet our production quotas for the month. But first, stand up if any of you have ever worked in an ESRP related role."

No one moved.

One of the prospective employees slowly raised their hand.

"Yes, go ahead."

"Umm, what does ESRP stand for?" he asked.

"Great question, it stands for Environmental Sustainability and Recovery Production. It means any working position that is related to producing something that contributes to Novolica's climate actions. Mining, energy, manufacturing for climate, any of those roles would be examples."

All nine people stood up.

Roger raised his hand.

"Another one, lay it on us."

"Umm, do you have any regulations against working under an alias here?"

The other eight employees all eyed him suspiciously. The foreman folded his arms. "Well, I suppose we could work something out. It's not the first time we've had this request. Assuming you pass the assessments and character interview."

Roger nodded curtly.

"Any other questions?" asked the foreman.

No one spoke.

"Excellent," the burly man said enthusiastically. Everyone was led to a separate area to assess their skills, then they were all hired and assigned roles.

CHAPTER TWENTY-ONE

Safety Mirage

It had been one month since Roger arrived in JX-VII. Working at Tortuga was enough to cover the stay at the Suenos Cumplidos Inn and feed himself. He also purchased an encrypted personal handheld to make and receive secure calls. He had not tried to reach Marela yet and it was starting to eat at him.

"Today will be the day," Roger said.

"Tonight when she's back home from work, I'll secure the line and call. We'll keep it short so there is no chance of someone getting my location."

After some hesitation, he dialed her number. It felt like hours had passed by as the connection was established.

"Hello, who is this?"

Roger's heart pounded fast.

"Marela, it's—it's me."

"OH MY GOD!" she cried out "You're ok. Dammit, I was so worried about you! What happened?"

"Before I say anything, it may not be safe," Roger warned. "Has anything suspicious been happening around you in the past few weeks? Have you been followed or received calls from anyone?"

"Yes, two days after you disappeared I—I was dismissed from my career and called in for an inquiry. All they wanted to know was where you were and if you had tried to contact me. Luckily you hadn't or I wouldn't be answering this call right now. But since then I haven't heard or seen anything abnormal. I came back to La Bajo to stay with Jolla. I figured we would be safer together here where there was a larger resistance already formed against the Prelicans. Their reach doesn't extend here so you can rest easy. I even got my handheld encrypted so we could talk in case you tried to contact me."

This put Roger at ease and he started recounting everything that had transpired since he left. He avoided specific details of his current whereabouts in case the call was intercepted.

"Wow, I'm so glad you're safe. Things are getting intense here. With your disappearance and the video now circulating all over Novolica, a lot more people are starting to distrust the Prelicans. Your approval score has been frozen since you disappeared. They are selling it as you no longer want to hold office as Chancellor. But you had gotten up to thirty-eight percent before the hold was put in place."

"THIRTY EIGHT PERCENT!" Roger yelled.

"Yes. There are a lot of people looking for you—from both sides right now. I'm glad you're altered, but we have to find a way for you to make another statement. If we can prove that you are alive and haven't given up they'll be forced to reopen the approval ratings. You would have a chance to take the Chancellor's place again."

"But how? I obviously can't show my real face and I definitely don't want people to find out where I am in case the ones that want to kill me find me first."

"I'll talk to Jolla. There has to be a way for her to get another message out for you. Let me get back to you in a few days. Will I be able to contact you again at this number?"

"No. I have been scrambling the identifier codes every few days. The only way we'll talk again is if I reach out to you directly."

Marela cleared her throat loudly. "What do you mean IF? IF you try to contact me. I haven't forgotten everything that happened between us. I can't imagine you not wanting to… or even me not…"

There was an uncomfortable silence.

"Ok. I'll contact you at this time in five days. Until then, we will keep the communication quiet to be safe."

"Please, take care of yourself Rog. I can't lose you too."

"I will. Talk to you soon."

Roger felt a strong surge of motivation.

People still support me. They're out actively looking for me to become their new Chancellor. My approval rating's up even outside of La Bajo.

Five days later, he contacted Marela again.

This time both she and Jolla were on the call to discuss their next actions.

"We have to give some kind of update," said Jolla. "The first video worked out great, but since then no one has seen or heard from you. The Prelicans have stated publicly that you must come out to declare yourself once again for candidacy. Only then will they re-open the approval ratings to make the scoring system valid."

"Yes, but it could very well be a trap," chimed in Marela. "They've already tried to get rid of him once. His entire declaration could be a ruse to figure out where he is. We have to find a way to do this without putting him in danger."

"Jolla, is there any way we could do another video release without meeting in person?" asked Roger.

"Well, maybe, but there is no way the quality would be as good. It would take me much longer to get it to an acceptable state to send out. And I thought you were altered—the last thing we want to do is show what you look like at this moment."

"AGREED," added Marela fervently.

"Well, my voice sounds the same, right? We could make this one an official audio only release. This way I can tell everyone what's happened without risking my current location or showing my face. You could add a voice detector to the clip, that way everyone sees a verification of my identity."

"That could work, but we would need a high tech audio capturer. For the clip to be uploaded to the hub channels it has to be high quality. I can send you a list of some models I would recommend. They should be available at any location that sells handhelds."

"Is there any chance someone would be able to find him with the voice capture we send out?" Marela asked. "After all, we'll be sending this to everyone and it will detail an attempt the Prelicans made to actually kill him. I want to know how big the risk is in this."

"We should be ok," Jolla assured her. "I can scramble the signal so no one knows where exactly it originally came from. It would be nearly impossible to find someone solely based on a voice capture that's been routed through hundreds of different channels. Roger, you'll just need to make sure to scramble the device you send the message from to protect both ends of the connection."

"Ok, let's do it," he said concludingly.

She sent the list of devices he could purchase to get the best audio quality. He didn't waste any time and re-visited the place where he had gotten the encrypted handheld.

"This one will do," he said as he selected one of the audio grabbers.

The next day, he finished his shift at Tortuga early and went straight to the land rover. He did not want to risk someone overhearing his recording. The land rover was sitting exactly where he'd left it when he arrived.

Inside, he made himself comfortable on the small blankets he had become so accustomed to sleeping on. He turned on the audio capture device and held it out in front of him.

"My name is Roger Allen Aimes. I—I uh, I'm alive and they tried to kill me. I want to keep being the Chancellor. I mean, I want to uhh, re-start the approval for Chancellor."

That sounds terrible. No way I'm playing that over again. Think for a moment.

Once again he held it out in front of him and started.

"My name is Roger Aimes. The same one you approved at over

twenty percent rating. Uhh— twenty percent positive rating for me to become your Chancellor. Prelicans almost killed me for the last video. So I ugh, I'm resigning. I mean—I am resubmitting for it."

He turned it off again.

I'm going to need to write something out.

He took notes on his handheld what he wanted to say word for word.

After hours of reading and re-reading and proofing and changing, he was satisfied. He grabbed the notes and flicked his finger upward to allow them to float boldly as a projection of the handheld in midair.

He started the recording. First by detailing how he had narrowly escaped the grasp of armed men after he was invited to reinstate himself for the approval ratings. Highlighting his previous revelations were still valid and that the Chancellor needed to be held accountable. Finally, he announced his intention to resubmit himself for approval and would only appear publicly when he knew it was safe for him to do so.

He painstakingly made himself listen to the recording over again to review. After two replays, he re-recorded it. Once he resolved that the new version was as good as it would ever be, he sent it straight to Jolla.

He leaned backward against the interior of the land rover, relaxing his tensed frame.

"I'll need to re-anonymize my number so this can't be tracked," he said to himself.

He checked the time on his handheld device.

"Oh shoot! I need to be back at work in four hours. No wonder Jolla hasn't responded yet. It's the middle of the night for her."

He left the rover and walked back to the inn. Once inside, he laid down and completely passed out before any more thoughts could find their way coherently into his mind.

～

ZIP ZUP ZOOM ZIP ZUP ZOOM ZIP ZUP ZOOM

Roger was abruptly woken up by the daily alarm he had set for work. He had not felt this agitated since he had arrived in town. He woke up with his long decoy hair matted and wrapped over his face.

Begrudgingly he threw both legs over the side of the bed. He felt a cold dry patch of slobber on the side of his face. Forcing himself toward the wash station, he couldn't help but feel stale. He tried to push the idea of going back to bed out of his mind.

"You're already awake. You are awake. It's time to get ready," he repeated to himself over and over.

His body went into autopilot as he willed himself forward.

He had to work overtime due to leaving early the day before. After work, he found himself still feeling as exhausted as he had when he left in the morning. It was a chilly, dark night. The clouds covered the sky with no moon anywhere in sight. He was alone, walking back to the inn in a dead silence.

As he wobbled about along the passway, he pulled out his handheld. Roger realized he hadn't checked it all day—his mind was consistently lost and wandering. He focused on the small lit display and looked at a notification that had been pending for hours.

Roger stopped in his tracks as he slowly read over the notes from Jolla several times.

06:28
GOT IT- Will setup the analyzer now

07:56
Worked perfectly with the analyzer, going to try to post it for the early morning hub releases today

10:52
We're a GO for today's hub release. Everyone will know you are still in it by the end of the day

13:54
The news feeds are blowing up! You've probably already scrambled this number by now but I wanted to tell you you did great. If

you're seeing this, the next time we talk in a few days—you'll be a candidate again

17:22
If this line is still open, get back to La Bajo as soon as you can. People here are talking about protecting you. Citizens everywhere are starting to speak out. I don't think it's safe for you alone with this kind of uprising happening

Roger's eyes widened.

Shit! The erase codes. I never anonymized the number after I sent Jolla the recording.

He fidgeted around in the dark when he heard rattling noises. It sounded like large vehicles moving on the main road. Roger looked back down at the handheld.

Are they coming for me?

He hurried in the direction of the inn. He tried vigorously to erase the handheld once again.

His pace sped up more and more until he was bouncing forward in a brisk trot. He had found the code he needed and was milliseconds away from erasing the device. The vehicles sounded slow but were moving in his direction.

He hopped forward moving as fast as he could without drawing too much attention to himself.

BAM- KLUNK.

He tripped over a large sharp curb on the passway that he had completely missed in the dark. His handheld flew out of his grip somewhere into the night. He doubled over on his side to recover from the pain now surging through his right leg and chest. The whirring sound was becoming more pronounced.

It's them! It has to be. No other everyday vehicle sounds like that. And it's getting louder.

He felt around frantically for the handheld.

"If I don't have the handheld, they can't track me!"

He abandoned the device as he forced himself to his feet, now moving swiftly in the direction of the inn. The closer he got, the more the sound of the machines surrounded him. The initial noise was still coming from behind him but another secondary loud grinding noise was now approaching or maybe even waiting—

"NO!" he called out.

Roger sprinted. Changing his direction from the inn toward the land rover's hiding place instead. His bag he carried to work was bobbing back and forth on his shoulder swinging wildly.

The more he ran the more pronounced the pain in his knee became. He was now down to a run-hobble-limp. He peered into the night to try and see how to get back to the land rover. He had not traveled to it while it was this dark. He passed a sign reading *40 KM into JX-VII.*

"Damn, I've seen that sign before. I've got to go the other way."

Roger took a sharp left, missed a step on his hobbled leg and skipped a few times on the other to catch his balance and steady himself. He didn't stop running and pressed on toward the land rover. His ears were ringing.

It got darker and darker. He ran on for another ten minutes and now he could hear himself breathing loudly with every step. Sweat poured from every strand of his knotted hair.

"Another sign," he said to himself as he could now make out a bright colored posting up ahead.

He willed himself over to it and hunched over, exhausted. Breathing heavily with strained exhales he picked his head up to look at the posting.

25 KM into JX-VII.

"No no no! I'm going the wrong way."

He took a few steps backward, realizing his mistake while also not entirely sure which direction was correct. He looked around in the pitch black and listened intently. He could now hear it again. The sound of the machines. Though he couldn't make out which direction they were headed. There was definitely more than one.

"Can't stop," he said between his heaving.

He doubled back toward the direction he came from. Now rapidly losing the energy to run, he was again relegated to brisk hopping. The pain in his leg was stronger than ever. Then he stopped.

Dead in his tracks. He could hear two separate vehicles more distinct now than ever. They sounded close.

A large silhouette appeared. Roger took a few steps backward.

"They don't know who I am. They won't know it's me."

At that moment, he heard an ear-piercing whizzing noise from behind him. Instantly, he was wrapped in a metallic cable. His arms and legs were bound together tightly as he was slammed onto the path in front of him. He felt an electric current coursing through his body jolting his every nerve.

He yelled out in excruciating pain. His limbs shook violently as the electricity penetrated to his bones.

"Analyze it now while he's screaming. That's got to be him. He dropped his handheld and took off running," called out a high-pitched voice. Roger wanted to stop himself, to resist but it was no use. There was nothing else he could do but scream as the intensity of the shockwaves increased.

"It's a match," yelled out another voice.

The current stopped jolting him, though his body still twitched uncontrollably. As he lay there stiff, teeth gritted tightly, both vehicles approached.

The group of pursuers closed in on him. In an instant he was kicked in the back and rolled over on his side. He counted five, no seven people in total now standing over him. He didn't say a word. His skin, now ice cold. His body trembling uncontrollably.

"We know it's you, Aimes, we've already confirmed your voice match," the first person called out.

She was short and plump. Roger felt the full force of her small, stout frame as she stomped down hard right on his stomach. He gasped loudly for the air that was avulsed from his body.

"He's been altered. Should we change him back first?" said a squeaky voice from behind.

"Naw, if we change him back everyone would know it was him we killed," this voice was much deeper than the others. The deep-voiced man yanked Roger upward by his hair.

"You would like everyone to see who you are now, wouldn't you, ya piece of shit."

Roger was pummeled with multiple fists directly to his mouth and eyes.

WHACK, another kick to his face.

CRACK, another kick to his side.

Followed by a hard fist to his throat. He lost track as painful blows hailed from all angles. The wires kept him tightly bound and he couldn't use his arms or legs to shield himself.

Time became blurred as Roger's consciousness faded. The dark of night was now turning a steamy shade of gray. His eyes partially closed and beginning to swell were rolling to the back of his head. He spattered blood from his mouth.

This is it.

PHEW, PHEW, PHEW

One of the attackers ducked for cover but the small woman who spoke up first was hit.

She fell hard right on top of Roger's brutally beaten body. The others looked around frantically to find the source of the long, sharp pointed needles that were flying their way. Another person was hit and fell backward this time adjacent to Roger. The remaining people still standing hurried toward their vehicles.

One more was hit and collapsed before the rest could get safely inside. Roger could hear them yelling frantically trying to figure out who had attacked them. Sitting completely still, the running sound of their machines filled the air.

Roger, barely conscious, tried to roll and turn around but there was no hope. Not only was his entire body throbbing but he now had one of his attackers laying across him.

A gust of wind filled the area as a power glider appeared. Two men approached, pushing the plump woman off of Roger and lifting him. A third body leaned out of the power glider and began firing some type of large weapon Roger had never seen before toward one of the vehicles. The armored transport started firing back at the glider that deflected everything it was hit with. One of them brandished a laser and cut off the attached wiring in an instant while tossing him into the glider.

"We got him! Let's get him to Danny."

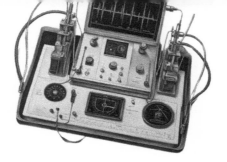

CHAPTER TWENTY-TWO

Rich Saviour

Roger awoke in an unfamiliar place. He lay in a large bed, battered and bruised all over. His breathing was raspy and painful. There were medical wrappings over his face and legs. An attachment to his arm funneled fluids through his body.

There was a mirror across the room from him. He tried to lift his head to look into it. He grunted loudly as his neck felt heavy and stiff. Boosting himself a tiny bit, he saw in his reflection that his alterations had been removed.

He sunk back deeply into the bed and slept again.

Roger was woken up by a presence looking over him. The figure was slim and bony. He had a thick red beard and short wisps of hair on his head. His eyes were piercingly blue with an icy stare that made Roger think he was looking directly through to his soul. Visibly older, he had deep wrinkles covering his face skin.

He moved over to the medical device and monitor that was connected to Roger. The man clicked a few buttons. After reading the monitor, he looked back at Roger and put a hand on his shoulder.

"Ya goin' t' be a bit of oolrigh' mate. Weren't sure if ya were goin' t' make it for a while there. Name's Danny Eurig. Ya sendin' out ya new welcome message unsecured like that was quite iffy. I reckon it took em less 'n an our to trace that one down. Lucky for ya a took a few sickies and had me guys watchin em right close. We know the hit squad when we see'm."

Roger looked confused. Danny understood.

"The Prellies, mate. They been lookin hahd for ya. Knew it was only a matt'r o' time before they went out t' finish d' job. But we was watchin em righ' close we were. Hop'n we could find ya before they did or get t' ya aftah they led the way, mate. Hadn't seen much activity for days till that message come round. In the nick o' time we were. The Prellies were whippin good on ya. No doubt would've pulled ya cahd but we showed up. Daam well pleased, you'll be fixed up 'n no time I tell ya."

"Why?" Roger said raspily.

He had been trying to muster enough strength to ask this question for some time. Every syllable that left his lips felt like iron grinding against metal. Danny looked back at him, surprised. He squeezed Roger's shoulder.

He looked him squarely in the eyes and muttered "Cause ya the fuutcha, mate. Get some res' now."

He clicked something on Roger's monitor before leaving him alone again. Without any resistance, Roger drifted back off to sleep. His body ached and his brain was tired.

A few days passed before Roger became fully conscious again. Some of the bruising on his face had healed. He could now move both of his arms though he still had a limited range of motion. He sat up in the bed and leaned over to one side to stand up.

Roger looked like he had been hit by a power glider. The pants he wore were tattered and his shirt had been removed. As he stood up, he winced and clutched his ribs in pain. He walked toward the slider where the man that had woken him up came through.

Roger slowly peered out into the corridor. The place was absolutely massive. It looked like an endless hallway in both directions and he had no clue which way to go to find his savior. He leaned against the wall to steady himself and started slowly down the corridor looking for someone, anyone. He passed another room that looked like an ancient book repository.

There were actually physical copies of books with a few workspaces scattered about. He saw another huge room that looked like an E-Raq court. There were six different headsets mounted on a wall and tons of different style controllers resting under them.

Who is this guy? This place must cost a fortune.

In the next open area was a high ceiling with lavish lighting. The floor was marble and had an image of a palace ingrained into it.

Through a window on the other side of the cavernous room, he could see a lush green landscape outside that looked like a scene from a vacation hub channel. He hobbled over to get a closer look.

"HEY!"

The shout came from behind. He heard someone walking fast toward him.

"How in the world did you get out of bed? The monitors didn't anticipate you being able to walk for another five to seven days."

The upset woman approached Roger. Her expression was serious, yet caring. She had freckles across her round face. Her dark toned hair was shortened on one side and the other side hung over part of her face.

"You should still be resting. My father will be worried if he sees you out of bed."

Roger steadied himself.

"So your father is… Danny?"

"Yes."

"But you… your accent sounds—"

"Yea, yea I speak like my mother. Now let's get you back to lie down, ok?"

She slowly guided him back to his room.

"Who is your father and where are we?"

"My father is one of the wealthiest men in Novolica. He owns Eurig Electronics."

Roger's eyes opened wide as he jerked sideways to look at her square-ly once again.

"No way! I've seen that logo everywhere, on shilohs and even on the heating system in my house. Your father owns the entire company?"

She nodded her head.

"No wonder this place is so huge."

"Right now we are in Onfroy. It's a wealthy region an hour outside of Leiton City," she continued.

Roger's stomach turned. She noticed his reaction.

"Don't worry, there's no way they can get to you here. We have some of the best equipment to prevent you from being tracked. The com-pound is also heavily guarded around the clock. You are completely safe."

Roger took a deep breath.

"Thank you. For saving me and allowing me to stay here. I didn't catch your name."

"I'm Priscilla." She smiled "The last of Danny's children."

"How many of you are there?"

"There *were* three of us. My youngest brother died when he was a teenager and the eldest we lost five years ago from an inquiry."

"I'm sorry to hear that."

She looked pained and did not respond. Roger left the topic alone.

They arrived back to where Roger's medical rest area was set up.

"I'll give you the full tour another time. For now, you need to get your strength back. We are all depending on you."

Roger gave her a sideways look.

"What do you mean?" he asked.

"We didn't save you because you were some innocent bystander. We knew you would be attacked and intervened to make sure you could finish the campaign. We want you to be the Chancellor."

She looked at him scrutinizingly. Roger did not respond to her out loud.

There's no way in hell I'm doing this anymore. They've tried to kill me twice now. Lucky, how lucky I am. I barely escaped death again. It was almost over.

He resituated himself in the bed and looked at the far wall.

"We are not going to let you give up," said Priscilla.

She nodded toward him before leaving the room.

Roger's mind swirled and he felt restless.

How will I end this? I have to tell them I'm not doing it anymore. Marela! I need to know she's ok.

That evening, Danny brought him dinner with solid food.

His first real meal since arriving. Roger had never seen such a spread. The large tray had an assortment of vegetables, various pieces of fish, fruits, and sauces.

"Eat up, mate," instructed Danny happily.

Roger nodded respectfully as he started to attack his plate the same way he was attacked not too long ago. He jabbed his utensils with purpose into the delicious items sitting in front of him. His mind felt more relaxed than it had been since he arrived. It felt like a large weight was lifted from his shoulders and the tense tightening of fear that had gripped him temporarily subsided.

Danny waited patiently until he finished his meal.

"Now then, ya all fed, we need t' talk about ya next release, mate."

Roger didn't want to look at him but he felt a daggering stare piercing through him. He turned slowly, and met Danny eye to eye.

"What makes you think I still want to be part of this? I've been almost killed twice now and nothing has been gained. No one has been helped."

Danny eyed him with a harsh gaze.

"Why do ya think they a' truyin t' off you? Because you're annoyin' them or ya told some information that loads of people probably already knew. No mate, they want t' off ya because you's threatenin' the very core of the system they built, and enough people agree with ya t' make that change happen. A change that is well overdue. They fear you Rogah. When someone like you comes along and can make a real difference and actually intend t' do what they claim of helpin' people. Pshh—in their eyes, no such person should exist. Now is not the time to stop, now we need to double down. Because they ah' gone to such great lengths and risked exposin' who they truly are, there is no better moment of time to step up and end the Prelican regime for good."

Danny spoke fiercely but with a consoling undertone. Roger held on tightly to each word he was saying. Though still apprehensive, he couldn't help but feel motivated again.

"I know things need to change. The system is broken. I never agreed to pay for the change with my life."

"Ya lost someone from an inquiry righ'? Someone close t' ya I'd imagine."

Roger paused, tears welling up in his eyes.

"My, my mother. It should have never happened."

"Oy lost me son, mate. Me oldest and last son alive. Heir to me whole empire. Ya met Prisc—she is amazing. But oy've raised ha, oy know ha bettah n' anyone. She doesn't want control of all of this. Ne-vah has."

Danny stepped away from Roger and looked out the window of the room. Finally he turned back around and faced Roger.

"There ah millions, mate. Millions who've had to endure this pain. Ya have the chance save people from sufferin'. They deserve it."

Images of his mother flashed before his eyes, and of others Roger had known, executed by mentir screenings. Still eyeing him intently Danny stood up tall and folded his arms. Roger took a deep breath in and exhaled slowly.

"Where do we start?"

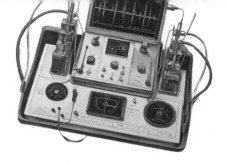

CHAPTER TWENTY-THREE

Surrender Off The Table

Five weeks passed since Roger was ambushed. His strength had returned. He began bonding with his saviors.

Danny owned hybrids and Roger took a liking to them almost instantly. Hybrids were created by breeding the last of a dying sheep population with horses. The new species kept their tall frames and muscular legs. They appeared docile with their thick, soft coats but their massive horns made them deadly.

The ones owned by Danny were always calm and happy, ready to be ridden by anyone that would give them food and attention.

Roger and Danny would ride the hybrids and talk for hours. Roger learned Danny had been placed in his career but took it upon himself to frequently work for other organizations in his free time. Eventually one of his volunteering organizations opened a leadership role just for him and tripled his wage to convince him to work there.

He took the higher level role and repeated this process until eventually starting his own company. Danny often expressed his discontent with the Restoration and talked about how he had seen dozens of coworkers and friends called in for inquiries to never return due to dubious and sometimes unjustly personal circumstances. As a result, he became a recluse, fearing human connection would get him killed.

They agreed getting Roger reinstated as a candidate would require several public declarations. With armed security and the use of a few decoy vehicles, Roger would be able to escape to safety while the news spread. Once people heard what happened to him, there would be overwhelming support and no choice but to reinstate him to full candidacy status.

Priscilla would organize three events, carefully constructing the logistics. A public announcement would be sent out eighteen hours before with details. The exact location of the event was to be disclosed after they arrived.

Given the dangerous and still very active risk against Roger's life, he decided not to communicate any of the planning to Marela. Though he longed to see her again, he knew bringing her closer would make her a target. Priscilla assured him that a quick handheld chat would be safe with their masking capability but Roger resisted.

For the first event, they would use power gliders and park them fifty kilometers away from the final location. Then take three e-vans the rest of the way. Priscilla mapped out multiple different routes.

Roger rehearsed his new speech every few hours and alternated reciting it to Danny and Priscilla. Priscilla gradually became annoyed with hearing the speech over and over. Danny welcomed it and gave suggested changes each time he heard it.

"Mate, ya right on the money. A tweak in this part and ya'll be fashioned t' suway the crowd."

Roger would pace back and forth through the long corridors speaking and imagining how the crowd would react. As the event date approached, he felt tingling sensations in the pit of his stomach. He knew he wanted to continue and there was no doubt in his mind that he would receive the support he needed. After everything that had happened to him, he knew it would only strengthen the resolve for other citizens to turn toward him.

On the day of the first event, the whole team was prepared. The security detail and transportation were laid out as Priscilla had planned.

Roger memorized his speech word-for-word.

He wore a formal overcoat and fine textured trousers that Priscilla had purchased for him. As they arrived at the first checkpoint location and exited the power gliders, he pictured himself out in the crowd.

Maybe Marela will find a way to show up. I miss her.

"Ok, here's the plan. You all take e-van 2 down route D. That way you will arrive at the site of the event fifteen minutes after us and e-van 3 will arrive only about five minutes after you. We'll sweep the area and let you both know once we've scouted a safe broadcast location. Remember, do not get out until e-van 3 has arrived and our scouting has finished," said Priscilla. She spoke with fierce determination as everyone nodded in agreement.

"I—I just want to say", stumbled Roger nervously, "I really appreciate everything you all are doing for me. Thank you so much. I know this isn't an easy task to–"

"Yes, of course Roger, we all want the same thing so don't worry about it for one second. A win for you is a win for all of us," interrupted Priscilla.

She flashed him a reassuring smile as they departed. Exactly how they planned, each e-van arrived separately to the rendezvous point. Once the first team had given the ALL CLEAR, everyone got out simultaneously. They looked like a well-formed unit as they walked in a rigid pattern keeping Roger at the center.

Priscilla was at the helm plotting their course. Her disguise completely hid her identity. Her typical short, dark hair was now covered with long blonde strands. Heavily tinted auto specs were covering her eyes and freckled face.

Her handheld device in front of her guided them.

"Ok, here goes the first wideband release. Roger, get ready for your closeup."

She turned toward Roger and with a big smile, pointed the handheld at him. The guards surrounding him moved out of view. Roger sucked in as much air as he could and squared his shoulders.

"I, Roger Allen Aimes, am still here. Despite numerous attempts against my life after submitting my candidacy for Chancellor, I am alive. Today I will address the citizens of Novolica on my own terms, at a time that we the people dictate.

We will be sending the location for anyone that wants to join me. I'll need each and every one of you to help boost my approval rating high enough to finally stop this never-ending pattern of unfairness and uncertainty we know all too well. Join me today, in one hour."

Roger felt himself sweating profusely. *I didn't think I would be this nervous.*

"It's done," said Priscilla approvingly. She tucked away her handheld and led them to the final location.

"I suspect people will be able to find us soon now that I've uploaded the coordinates."

Hearing Priscilla say this caused Roger to glance around at the protectors he now had at every side of him. There were seven enormous individuals towering over him with bulging arms and legs. They were wearing tight clothing that accentuated their muscles. Each of them were armed with shockers to neutralize anyone that came too close.

After an hour had passed, people began arriving at the location. First a few dozen that quickly turned into hundreds of people circling the area and eagerly waiting for his announcement. Though there was no stage, the area they were waiting in was sloped and had a building at the top of it with large columns opening out into the air. Here is where Roger would stand and make his address. The slope made it easier to prevent people from getting close to him.

Some tried approaching to greet him which was swiftly shutdown by his protectors. Though he still smiled and waved to acknowledge everyone. As he glanced out into the growing audience, Roger had hoped to see a familiar face. He pictured Marela running up to him and embracing him. They had not spoken in weeks and he couldn't stop thinking about her.

Everyone was now fixated on him. The eager crowd waited patiently to hear what he would say.

After an hour had passed, Priscilla signaled to Roger to speak. She reached inside of a utility bag and found a voice amplifier.

Roger focused on the words he had memorized to address the audience. He stood up tall and walked up to the highest point of the slope in front of the pillars. The audience quieted.

"My fellow Novolicans, I know it has been months since I was last in front of you. Today I stand, more determined than ever. More determined, more committed, more empowered. My life was spared for this moment, our moment.

"There have now been two attempts to murder me behind the scenes. The first time was after I released the video detailing Chancellor Prumpt's deceit of his mentir screenings. After I was invited to Leiton City to re-declare myself as a candidate, I was attacked and narrowly escaped their grasp. The second time, an entire team was sent to assassinate me while I was under disguise.

"Despite these events, I will not give up. In order to save the lives of the people we care most about. To spare our children, our loved ones, and our closest companions the pain that we've all known. The fear we've all felt of stepping into those inquiry rooms, knowing we may never leave. In that split second, these cold metal killing machines can determine whether or not we live or die.

"We can put a stop to this. After being selected as your Chancellor, the first thing I'll do is end the mentir mandate. No longer should we have to mourn people before it's their time to go. We were all promised a better society by using these machines on one another. Yet, the people who put the mandate into place aren't even abiding by their own rules. Why should we be the only ones to suffer?

"The Restoration plan has failed us. Our nation is broken because of this. Today I'd like to share with you all how we can build Novolica back together. So that all citizens have a fair chance at life, not just a select few. Once I'm Chancellor of Novolica, we will

RECONCILE our country. We will make it equitable for everyone and rebalance the power that has been usurped from us as citizens by the Prelicans. Our only way forward is together. And together, we will enact the Reconciliation Mandate to put an end to mentir screenings once and for all!"

Roger was cheered with raucous applause. The audience chanted "Reconciliation" with fists pumped in the air. As the chant grew louder and louder, tears began to swell in Roger's eyes.

Priscilla informed everyone the first event had concluded and that they would be announcing the next event soon.

Immediately after, the guards circled Roger. People were trailing behind as the group stepped hastily toward the transport vehicles. Everyone was on high alert, still moving tightly in their protection formation. When they arrived at their transports to take them back to the power gliders, the guards guided Roger in first and glanced around to ensure they were not being followed.

"Looks like we're all clear," said Priscilla. "You take route A, we'll catch up to you on route C."

She gestured to the remaining guards to leave in the last e-van on route B. Without hesitation the team piled into the transports and took off in opposite directions. One of the members of the team was now re-watching Roger's speech on his handheld. The story was already plastered throughout the hub stations. Spectators and hubcasters commented on his reemergence into the spotlight.

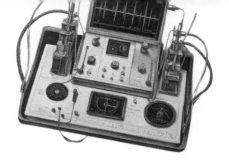

CHAPTER TWENTY-FOUR

One Last Push

"Any word from the Chancellor yet, or any of his Prelican cronies?" asked the driver.

"Not a peep," responded the guard with the handheld still showing Roger on the hub.

Roger's group was the second e-van to arrive at the rendezvous point. The van carrying Priscilla had not arrived. The two groups waited for the others before getting in the power gliders. After two hours of waiting, no one spoke. Not a single word was uttered. Everyone looked out the windows constantly, surveying the area.

Each designated route was thirty minutes from the power gliders. They had been instructed to only contact one another during the transit process in the case of an absolute emergency. This way, their communications couldn't be traced. Another forty-five minutes passed before a rumbling noise echoed in the distance. The third e-van appeared.

"It's them!" yelled Roger.

He motioned toward the slider to exit the e-van before one of the guards grabbed his wrist firmly and pulled it from the handle. He looked at him and back over to the approaching transport.

"Have to make sure it's really them first and they are safe. Someone could've forced them to reveal our location."

Roger nodded in agreement.

Please be them. I can't bear anyone getting hurt because of me.

The vehicle parked directly beside the transport that Roger was sitting in. The slider opened and the team jumped out frantically, Priscilla last. Roger and his group all came out.

"What happened?" asked the driver as he shut the slider behind him.

"We picked up a tail," said Priscilla hurriedly. "And they were good, it took us forever to lose them. It's possible they could still be on their way here. We have to go NOW!"

There were no more questions. Roger's team immediately smushed him into one of the power gliders and hastily sealed it behind them. In seconds, both power gliders vanished into the sky.

After arriving back at the estate, Priscilla told Danny about their team being followed.

"Haa, wow those buggahs don't waste 'ny time do they. Crikey, we must be on the righ' trek. Couldn't have gone bettah, I tell yas."

The response to the announcement had proven Danny's point. People all over Novolica demanded the polls be reopened. Many echoed Roger's words for a reconciliation of the nation.

"Well things will get more challenging from here," chimed in Priscilla. "Now we are fully back into the public eye and everyone knows we have another event planned. I imagine they'll come up with a counterplan."

They had a few weeks to prepare for the next address and did not waste any time doing so. Roger created his new speech, Danny ordered more decoy transports to confuse anyone attempting to intercept them, and Priscilla narrowed potential locations and routes.

The planning for the second event had been much more intense than the first. Priscilla did not appreciate the fact that they were still followed. In response, she had found a location with hidden escape routes.

Instead of walking in plain sight to the vehicles, they would be

utilizing the service tunnels located in Finca. Danny contacted a mining contract liaison he knew to secure a map of all the tunnel access
points throughout the city.

"I cannot believe this many tunnels were there all along. The route
practically runs right under my old pod," shouted Roger in disbelief.

"No one uses them anymore, they're mostly from before the Restoration War," responded Priscilla.

Five days away from the event, hub channels discussed Roger's next
address. Everyone in Novolica was eager to see where his campaign
would end.

The additional vehicles had arrived, new transport e-vans and un-
identifiable, untraceable power gliders. A few of the guards were directed to go and place the e-vans at the location the power gliders
would land. They also placed vans around the city as decoys. After
arriving via power glider, there would be a short ride in the e-van to
each tunnel entrance to leave the site of the address.

Priscilla also came up with the idea of everyone wearing the same
clothing. This way even if someone managed to deduce where they
were going, they still would not know which group was the one to
follow to get to Roger. The plan was thorough and every precaution
was in place.

Roger, Priscilla and Danny spent hours every day with each other.
Danny shared his wisdom about his business and running his company. Roger listened intently and admired him greatly. The more time
they spent together, the more Danny became like a father figure to
him.

He urged him to get in touch with Marela saying that they were safe
and that there would be no risk. Danny could see how much Roger
thought about her and eventually had to try and hold back from mentioning it seeing how much anguish it caused him. Three days before
the event, all the clothing arrived.

"Oyem just glad I won't be there with ya buggers, those dacks are
hideous," laughed Danny.

Roger held up the tracksuit that was labeled for him. It had long sleeves and was an off-white color. There was one large stripe of yellow running diagonal across the chest which aligned with an equally thick and misplaced stripe down the pants. The sleeves were tightly fitted until they reached the cuffs where it bowed out awkwardly like the puffer ends of a makeshift magic trickster robe. The pants had a similarly flawed design with the ankle parts fluffing out widely at the end of a tightly fitted inseam. He pulled out the hood that was tucked into the top portion. It was a full face covering with a see-through front.

"These will keep us camouflaged amongst crowds. The entire group will put these on before walking to the broadcast area and again when we leave. This way, they won't know who to follow if they manage to tail any of us. We need to remember to take them off during the event so no one catches on," Priscilla mandated.

Everyone begrudgingly agreed given the enhanced security it would provide.

Finally, the day arrived. They were back in the power gliders and headed toward Finca. Once they got close enough, everyone put on their suits over top of their clothing, pulled the hoods down, and zipped them so their faces were unrecognizable.

The three power gliders veered off in different directions, landing near the transport vans. They then took the e-vans to the tunnel entrances. Roger's group had the longest distance to cover underground which intentionally made them the last to arrive after everyone else was in place.

The tunnels were forty meters deep in some areas and densely packed with moss and overgrown kudzu covering the walls and much of the paths. Down here, there were no handheld signals so each group had to rely on paper maps.

Each tunnel had lighting lines that hung from the top of the inner walls. Most lights had been broken or fallen into disarray, making it too dark to see. Each group had been given high powered flashlights to avoid getting off track. The taller people had to duck down and crouch to maneuver through tighter spaces. One of the guards in Roger's group had to be held up after experiencing light headedness and dizziness. The air in the tunnels was constrained making it hard to breathe.

Everyone navigated the dizzying tunnels that smelled of rot.

Priscilla's group approached an intersection, turned left, and moved forward until they came to another splitting path. Fifteen minutes after their descent, they had reached the exit ladder and resurfaced in the middle of town near an old rundown power plant.

They carefully opened the manual slider and exited one by one, now wearing their matching jumpsuits and appearing identical to one another. They shuffled in unison to the event location. The address was to be made public once everyone got to the rendezvous point.

The second group of all guards questioned every path they came across in the tunnels. No one had taken the lead like in Priscilla's group and Roger's group. Everyone rotated the paper map between one another to confirm the correct route.

They arrived at an area where groundwater had seeped into the underground maze. Their suits stopped the water from soaking them as they waded knee deep in runoff. They tried desperately to keep the map from touching the water fearing that it would quickly make their only guide to safety illegible.

After twenty-five minutes of sloshing heavily, they approached a steep stairway that led to an opening with glimmers of sunlight. They hurriedly climbed, eager to get back to the surface level.

At the top of the stairway, they noticed a crowd of individuals entering a small restaurant a short distance from them. The entrance to the stairway they had climbed was tucked behind a few old street transformers that were no longer in use. They stealthily weaved in and out of the large machinery to avoid being seen and found Priscilla's group waiting at the meeting point.

Roger's group struggled the most. Not only was one of the group members now being fully supported by two people, they constantly had to maneuver his body lower and turn him sideways to traverse the more narrow corridors.

They walked single file and sideways as the walls closed in on them. Their arms scraped against the concrete walls over and over as they pushed through the tight spaces. Roger looked at the map to see how much longer to the tunnel exit.

Their pace was slow and they awkwardly rotated who was supporting the injured group member as the fatigue set in. Roger stopped to examine the map more closely. At some point, he even resolved to turn it upside down which made everyone nervous. He flipped the map back right side up and looked intently at the walls to his left and right.

"According to this," he said, "our exit should be somewhere around here. Either it's directly in front of us, or we've walked right past it."

"How the hell are we so close and missed it? We can't see any exit. It's obvious you're reading it wrong," said the weakened guard.

Roger tried hard to ignore this as he rubbed his hand across the wall over a more darkened area than the rest. His fingers ran across a deep groove.

"HERE IT IS!" he called out loudly.

He pushed his hand deep into the indent and felt a handle. He shifted it loudly and some type of old mechanical slider was activated. Roger pushed into it hard, revealing a steep mud hill behind it leading back to the surface.

The group groaned loudly. The guard being supported threw his hands in the air and smacked his face, looking at the steep hill. They moved forward scaling the hill, digging deep into the mud.

Trying desperately to catch their breath, each of them gasped loudly for the clean oxygen of the open air now filling their lungs. A stark contrast from the muggy thin air in the tunnel. Their matching white jumpsuits now stained with the dark chunks of wet earth.

At last, they reached the top and could see the rendezvous point where there were a large number of people waiting for them in the same white fluffy suits they were wearing. After seeing one of them being supported, the other group members ran over to assist. Roger headed toward Priscilla.

"Why did you choose that path for us? It was terrible."

"Everything is going exactly according to plan, we've all made it here and we are only ten minutes from the site."

The rest of the group was now huddled together. Priscilla pulled her handheld from her pocket and moved East toward a set of buildings. They found a discarded street traveler lying alongside the expressway onto which their injured teammate happily boarded to not have to depend on anyone supporting his weight any longer. As they approached the location, Priscilla turned toward Roger and started walking backwards.

"Are you ready for your closeup, Mr. Aimes?"

Roger steadied himself, rubbing his palms down the sides of his legs to dry them.

"Wait, shouldn't we remove the suits? No one is supposed to know this is what we're escaping in right?" responded Roger.

"Oooh, good catch! Let's wait until we get to the actual broadcast area, then change back and make the announcement."

The broadcast location Priscilla had chosen this time was an old outdoor amphitheater that hadn't been used since Finca became the primary source of power for Novolica decades ago. It had fallen into disarray with grass and weeds growing out of the concrete blocks.

There were dozens of rows in tiers with eight different seating zones side by side. There was plenty of space for a large crowd. Roger surveyed the area to figure out where he would speak.

Priscilla moved forward with sending out the announcement once they were all in place and everyone had taken off their fluffy white jumpsuits.

Within twenty minutes of the announcement release to the local hub networks, people began arriving. No one was allowed to exit the bottom of the staircase to get close to Roger or the speaker area and the security personnel made sure of that.

Priscilla tucked herself away and out of sight from the general public. Roger took center stage in the speaker area.

He stood patiently, looking out at the growing crowd with his hands clasped firmly in front of him. The audience had swelled to a few hundred attendees who applauded after seeing Roger. He waved to everyone with one large sweeping motion of his hand from left to right.

"People of Novolica! I'd like to welcome you all to my home. Here, where I was assigned a career just like all of you. Here where I've worked in service to my nation for the past eight years. And in those eight years, not a day has gone by that I haven't feared for my life. Not only my life, the lives of my family, my closest friends, my—one true love. Because of the inquiry system, we all live in fear.

"Yet, perhaps we found some comfort in knowing that we all share this fear together as a nation. Comfort in knowing that everyone had to obey these same rules, to make it worth it for us all. Now we know better. Now we know that the very same leaders who put this system in place and have bound us to it do not share the same fear that we do. They don't have to fear, because they've made it so the rules and standards we live by don't apply to them. They live free, while we suffer in bondage.

"We need to end this. We should be free. We deserve the chance to live. Together, we can end this system of bondage we've been trapped in. We need to force the candidate approval system back on. The Restoration laws clearly state that a candidate can be voted in if the people approve them. I will be your candidate and end this oppressive system Chancellor Prumpt has doomed us to. Help me, citizens of Novolica. Help me reconcile our nation and force the candidate approval system. Because today, in this moment right now, we choose to live free."

A loud, thunderous boom of approval erupted over the crowd as Roger bowed slowly and waved to the crowd once again, indicating his departure. He retreated to behind the staging area where Priscilla had been watching. He took a few deep breaths. Priscilla's face was flush with excitement.

"You did an excellent job," she praised.

She showed Roger the front display of her handheld.

"They've done it! Your public approval rating has been reinstated. There are already recordings of what you said available on national hub networks. I suspect a vote will be held after the next announcement."

Upon hearing this, Roger's face lit up.

Only one more event to go. Then we can change things for good.

The security personnel guided Roger and Priscilla out of the area. As a unit, they hustled a few meters away in order to redeploy with their matching jumpsuits away from the view of the crowd. Once everyone had the uniforms back on, and faces completely covered, they split into two groups and headed toward the tunnel entrances hidden nearby in order to carry them back to the power gliders.

Priscilla and Roger were now in the same group, being led by one of the guards. After fifteen minutes of hustled trotting, they reached the ladder leading to the exit and climbing up one by one. As they appeared, the guards scanned the area. With no one in sight, they moved toward the e-vans, riding a short distance to the first power glider. Once they arrived, they found the first group waiting for them. With jumpsuits still on, they piled quickly into the two power gliders and were off in an instant, into the bright sky above.

CHAPTER TWENTY-FIVE

Rich Sacrifice

The public response to the latest announcement was immense. Roger's popularity skyrocketed throughout all of Novolica. The polls had officially been reopened and his approval rating was made public again.

This time, the rating had not fallen below thirty-eight percent. The Chancellor was forced to acknowledge Roger's political movements. He argued across every hub channel available that the inquiry system protected everyone's civil rights and made Novolica the great nation it is today.

He also harshly denied claims that he could beat mentir detectors. Not everyone took Roger's side and many still heavily opposed any change to the mentir protections that had been put in place.

"People are afraid, mate", said Danny one day as they were all listening to one of the Chancellor's speeches on the hub. "Ya can't expek the world t' turn ovah in a day."

"That's right," agreed Priscilla. "We've convinced a lot of people this system is wrong. The rest have to see for themselves. They've latched on so tightly to how things are, they can't imagine Novolica being any other way."

"Who am I to want to change the way people see their country?"

"Oi, we've been ovah this one ya. Oy believe in ya, 'alf the world agrees with me, things ah at a righ' time for change. We support ya all the way, mate. It's not just those o' lives ya savin, it's their rug rats for generations that'll be happy ya savin em. Not t' mention that Chancellor's a mongrel. It's righ' time everyone sees him cleah."

Priscilla nodded in agreement with Danny's words.

"Thank you Danny. I — I'm not sure I would have been able to finish this without you. We only have one more event left to broadcast, then we call for the election. We are almost there," said Roger with rising confidence.

"Speaking of that, I've already started planning," Priscilla added. "This event has to be the biggest one yet, and have the most space to accommodate a bigger crowd than before. They get larger every time and for this one, I feel we'll need to bring more security. Given the state of things and how close we are to getting the Chancellor out of his position—if there was a time things would be more dangerous, that time is now. I don't want us underestimating the measures the Prelican party would take in order to remain in power. You are doing a great job, Roger, and I personally feel the atmosphere with all of the citizens is changing. I can feel a different presence now when you are speaking and it's coming across on the hub channels as well."

Priscilla took a few steps back, folding her arms. She bit her bottom lip and stared intently. Finally, she blurted out, "I think we should have the final event in two weeks."

"How? There is no way," asked Roger, perplexed. "The last event was only three days ago. Why would we rush like that?"

"It's like I said. Given all of the attention this is getting, the Chancellor's becoming unhinged. He's been saying things on the hub channels that don't make much sense, or rather more than usual. And the latest rhetoric is so far from reality, there's no end in sight. The more desperate he gets, the more dangerous this will be."

"All the more reason we should plan carefully and not rush into anything, I would think."

"We can do it, we've already had two successful events and without any serious threats. Now is the time to finish it and get Prumpt out of sight and out of mind before he really does something that will damage Novolica forever."

Danny had managed to stay quiet throughout as he pondered the options.

"Mate, I think she's righ'. It's time oy endorsed ya publicly. With my influence added on the announcement of the third event. Crikey, it's brilliant."

Roger's last hope of delay had withered away. He had normally agreed with Danny on these things and he knew he'd be powerless to resist them both.

Taking advantage of the moment of epiphany, Priscilla added, "We'll need to make the announcement tomorrow, Da." She turned toward Danny. "It will give everyone time to anticipate the event and be ready to cast their votes on the day of. After your announcement, the Prelicans will probably deduce that Roger's been staying here so we need to increase our security. At the press conference tomorrow, you'll have to go ahead without the two of us and have your business constituents present to show a united front."

"Good on ya. Oyl sed it up."

Roger relented and they moved forward to planning the final announcement event in two weeks time. Priscilla followed her usual flow, scouting the perfect location and various entry and exit points. She constructed the event layout and where the audience would be situated.

Danny had called a public hubcast to announce the next event and his endorsement for Roger. On the day of the public hubcast, Danny was jittery. Priscilla commented on how he had not had a public hubcast in years but that the comfort would come back to him.

"You used to do these every three months for the business. I remember most of your addresses and most importantly, I remember how they made everyone feel. The constituents looked forward to hearing you provide the updates," Priscilla consoled.

Danny waived this off. Despite his nervousness, the hubcast was a success. He instantly garnered the attention of a multitude of hub channels given his stature in the business world. He was asked questions by hub representatives like "How long have you known Roger Aimes?" and "At what point did you start to think Roger Aimes has what it takes to be Chancellor?" Danny answered every single one of them flawlessly and with the same poise he always showed when advising Roger.

That night, Roger, Priscilla, Danny, and his staff all celebrated together.

There were five days until the final event. Priscilla made sure this one would be the biggest and most successful. She had gone over every detail from beginning to end. This time, he would call for the final vote.

Now that the approval system had been opened for everyone's handhelds, the final vote was inevitable. After a formal vote, they were confident Roger's votes would pass those of the Chancellor's, and Prumpt would finally be removed.

Roger felt more confident than ever. He knew in five days, his speech, his presence would be changing the world. He wasted no time drafting what he was going to say. He wrote, and edited, and wrote, and re-read over and over again. Roger was determined that this final address would be his best one yet. The next morning, after waking, the first thing he did was grab his handheld and read over every adjustment he had made the day before.

He read the entire speech aloud again to himself. He then found himself smiling. The speech was ready and he was now more excited than ever.

Danny can help me put the finishing touches on it.

He hurried to the kitchen to find him.

He found Priscilla standing with her arms folded behind Danny. Her posture was abnormally erect, too stiff. Danny was sitting, holding up his handheld high with his face scrunched, lips pursed tightly together.

The room was silent. Roger approached slowly. Priscilla turned to him as he moved closer to see what was happening. He could now see her eyes were floating in a pool of water about to overflow. He was taken aback.

"What's going on?" Roger asked.

No one answered. Not one word.

Finally Danny responded in a dark laughing voice, "Haa hoo, the mongrols have played out their hands. Oye've been called in foor an inquiry."

Roger's chest pumped rapidly.

"How is that possible? You have not been anywhere nor seen anyone outside of the people in here since I've been here for the past few months. Who would have been able to submit you for an inquiry?"

"The Chancellor, that's who!" bellowed Priscilla.

The pools of water surrounding her eyeballs had finally runneth over, tears now flowing freely down her cheeks.

"That asshole. He saw the public announcement Danny made in support of the campaign and he took action. Maybe he figures if Danny doesn't- didn't…" Priscilla paused for a moment, hyperventilating to try and calm herself.

"With Danny out of the way, we won't have funding for the event—"

"Or security to protect us," Roger finished the thought for her.

She nodded in agreement.

"But we all know that no one can submit someone for an inquiry they have never met before. It's completely against the mandate," continued Roger.

"That's why oye'm gunna request t' name of moy submittah. Whatevah happens, oye'll send it to ya's both before oye go in."

He could not skip the screening. The Prelicans would have cause to search his personal residence, possibly finding Roger. A lump formed in Roger's thrat. He felt like he was straining to breathe.

This can't be happening. Not again.

Roger looked at Priscilla. She was wiping her face frantically, still trying to steady herself. He wanted to hear something from someone. From anyone, guidance, words of wisdom, or any type of direction.

What if Danny doesn't make it back? NO—don't! Don't think it. Dammit.

He felt a cold wave of emotion come over his body and he trembled.

Danny looked over and wrapped an arm around his shoulder. Priscilla joined them as they all embraced.

∼

The next morning, Danny was awake before anyone else. He didn't say anything, he didn't eat anything. Not long after eight am, he was off to his inquiry.

Getting to Leiton City was a breeze in his power glider. After finding a landing location, he strutted through the main slider of the inquiry office. Today it looked almost deserted. There weren't any guards waiting, nor the typical line of people hovering about the outside of the building, wondering if the day would be their last. Danny walked straight to the lobby and shouted.

"AY, ya's betta get out here before oy change me mind."

He pressed a buzzer that was sitting across from the waiting space. Within a few seconds, four large framed individuals appeared in the lobby. They approached Danny swiftly. The first one wasted no time grabbing Danny by the arm. He forced him toward the back while the others surrounded him.

"So who's called me in then? As a citizen, oy've got the righ' ta know."

Danny made an abrupt movement, wrenching away from the grip of his captor and swiftly moving his fingers to his pocket.

"That's not negotiable."

The men surrounded him and two of them chuckled.

"You've been called in by the Chancellor, you imbecile. He's provided a statement for you. So let's say, your rights are going to be non-existent here pretty shortly."

With these last words, the guard swung a large fist at Danny hard into his side. Danny leaned over, wincing at the amount of air that had been forced out of his body. The other two men took advantage of the moment—elbow to the back, kick to the leg.

In an instant, Danny's body started to seize up all over and he was now being dragged back into the inquiry room. He felt himself being shoved into the cold metal seat as the clamps of the X3 Jig were strapped tightly on both forearms. The icy, dark room filled with the deep booming laughter of his captors. The floor was still stained from the last individual that didn't pass their inquiry. As the razors of the device hugged tightly across his forearms, Danny was not sad. Nor did he appear to be in anguish.

"What's me statement, gents?"

One of the men fumbled around for a sheet of paper in his pocket. He pressed a button on the X3 jig attached to Danny's arm and read aloud, "You've agreed to help a citizen of Novolica break the law by wrongly misguiding the public about the Chancellor. Do you accept or reject this statement?"

"Ha, absolutely reject mate—now start t' clock."

The man tossed the paper to the side and pushed another button on the X3 jig. He grinned as it began beeping.

Danny spoke loud and clear, "Oy've helped a citizen of Novolica expose the truth of ya bogan Chancellah."

As he stopped talking, the machine let out a loud squealing noise. Yet, he wore his signature smirk across his face and whispered lightly to himself:

"Thanks to ya," before his skin was sliced open and his life force, stolen. Never to return.

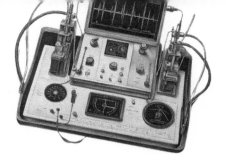

CHAPTER TWENTY-SIX

People First

Roger and Priscilla were devastated. They received a recording from Danny. His last message unequivocally confirmed that the Chancellor had been the one to request his inquiry.

He and Priscilla played the message back twice but could no longer bear it beyond that. The message did not stop with the confession from the Prelicans. It was running during Danny's entire time there. They heard his screams as the X3 jig bore down on him.

They could hear his body tremble and the ones who detained him laugh through it, insulting him. The disrespect didn't stop once he had been confirmed dead. The recording continued to run as they unclamped his lifeless body from the machine.

Sounds of urination and his body being tossed into the recycler echoed, all while the Prelicans were degrading Danny and Roger's campaign. Furious anger coupled with a deep sadness swept over Priscilla and Roger.

Once they determined there was no mistaking the incriminating evidence on the handheld, they released it to the public. The full, unfiltered message, forty-two minutes in length illustrating Danny's setup, death, and disposal.

It didn't take long after the message was released for Chancellor

Prumpt to be called to a public trial. It was against the Creed of the Reformation to call an inquiry against someone you have never met. Though the Chancellor would undoubtedly try to prove somehow that he had met Danny, the remainder of his public support had fully eroded.

The active polls pitting Roger against the Chancellor swung widely in the opposite direction. Roger's approval had gone up to eighty-nine percent while the Chancellor's dwindled to eleven percent, not even enough for him to be considered a candidate any longer.

The truth and the horrors of the inquiry system were unveiled for everyone to see and no one wanted any part of it anymore.

Two weeks later, Roger was requested to come to the capital city and accept the title as Chancellor of Novolica. The first person he called after receiving the message from officials was Marela.

He hadn't heard her voice in so long and when she answered, tears poured from his face, soaking his handheld device. She had longed to hear his voice and agreed to join him in the capital to see him accept the role of Chancellor.

Roger remained in Danny's estate even though Priscilla was absent. She'd left to spend some time alone. He wanted to let her grieve but needed her to be there in the capital with him.

The day before the inauguration, Priscilla returned to the estate and greeted Roger. It was cold and standoffish compared to how they normally greeted one another. Roger looked at her, puzzled.

"Did something happen while you were gone?"

"Yes. I was off tending to my father's affairs. He runs a multi-billion plinko valued company and his estate needed to be settled. Naturally as the only remaining heir, I should have been granted access to everything and given full ownership of the business."

Her eyes narrowed after saying this and her voice turned into grunt.

"And that did not happen. He's named you in his final will and entitled you to a fifty percent stake in the company, making you a part owner."

Roger's jaw dropped. He was completely dumbfounded.

"I don't know what to say—I, I didn't know."

He took a few steps backward and sat down on the nearest chair.

"It's already done," continued Priscilla. "I've decided not to dispute my father's last wishes. You are now a billionaire and an integral part of Eurig Electronics. We'll have to announce this to the constituents tomorrow after the ceremony."

"But Priscilla, how on Earth am I going to help run the company while being the Chancellor of Novolica?"

Her eyebrows nearly raised off the top of her forehead hearing this. Her eyes softened.

"Well, it would be nearly impossible. If you want to forfeit your stake, I will take care of everything."

Roger looked down at the floor and took a few deep breaths.

"Yes, but that's obviously not what he wanted," he forced out after a long pause. "Would that truly be what you would want as well? To be the sole head and public figure of Eurig Electronics, known all around the world?"

All of the remaining color left Priscilla's face. Hearing this did not make her feel better.

"Why would he leave you with such a large role knowing you would become the Chancellor? You don't know anything about the business and I've been alongside him my entire life." She began to sob. "It's true. I hate the spotlight. My father always knew. I want to be angry but, inside I feel relieved. I'm not sure how we'll manage this."

Roger did not have an answer for her. They sat in silence and tried to find reason in Danny's last wishes. Reasons that would never be confirmed or denied. They resolved to let it be for now.

The next day, people from all over Novolica gathered to celebrate and witness the role of Chancellor being passed on to someone else. It had been forty years since the Restoration occurred and many did not know what to expect from this new regime.

Prumpt had been disgraced and called all kinds of names, "hypocrite" always among them because of breaking the mandate he created. Roger was introduced onstage as the final candidate for the role of Chancellor and summoned to the front to speak and accept the role.

Marela had been clasping his hand tightly. He had to pry his hand from her before walking up. He spoke about what led to these events and the painful system of mentir inquiries.

He spoke of the importance of trust and understanding amongst one another to prevent something like this from happening again. He spoke of the reconciliation period to reduce the divide amongst citizens and uniting to create the best version of Novolica possible.

The crowd applauded loudly.

"Also, I want to disclose that I have been named as the Co-Executive Owner of Eurig Electronics. The global enterprise that was led to success by my dearest mentor and friend, Danny Eurig. Given the responsibilities required of me in this new role, as my first order of business I will be creating the role of Vice Chancellor. I will be appointing Marela de Nichols to the role of Vice Chancellor to help oversee the reconciliation of Novolica."

Roger motioned over to Marela.

She stood up with both hands covering her mouth. Her eyes were wide with astonishment.

He beckoned her to come forward. She felt frozen in place momentarily until an official ushered her to Roger's side so everyone could see. Looking out into the massive audience, she paused briefly. In the time she was able to collect her thoughts, she accepted the role of Vice Chancellor.

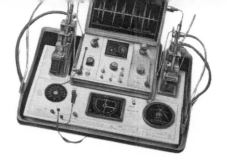

Epilogue

A curly haired woman sat behind a large desk in front of a bright window. She scribbled a few notes onto the electronic display, reciting words under her breath.

A quiet knock at the slider startled her. "Yes, come in," she called.

Roger Aimes walked into the large office, his hair now finely cut and donning an exceptionally crisp suit. As he pulled a handled from his pocket, a bright silver ring shimmered on his finger.

"Cutting it close aren't we?" he said as entered the room smiling.

Marela stood up from her seat and looked out the open window.

"I want everything to be perfect. You know how I get."

Roger approached in front her, blocking her view of the outside. He wrapped his arms around her tightly.

"Mrs. Aimes, if perfect was ever attainable, I have no doubt in my mind you would be the one to discover it."

Marela embraced her husband, resting her cheek on his chest.

"I don't want to assume they will elect me. You never know, someone could submit themselves. Make a play for chancellor instead. It's not unheard of. There's still a lot of work to be done. I just wonder, if they truly trust me without taking an inquiry."

"We've all found new ways to build trust with one another without the threat of being killed. The entire country has been just fine. We've adjusted. We owe all the progress to you. You've spent much more time in this office than me. Everyone in the whole world knows it."

Roger kissed her lightly on the forehead.

"You'll make a great chancellor, Muffin," he said smiling.

"Ah-Ah, watch it. Please make sure you don't accidentally say that when you announce me on stage."

She frowned for a moment before grabbing his hand and walking toward the slider.

"C'mon Mr. Aimes, we've got another election to win together."

Marela De Nichols Aimes was unanimously voted in as Chancellor of Novolica. The statute she had enacted for five-year terms in office was upheld by the Reconciliation National Agreement. After her time in office, she joined the judicial committee to play an active role in the fair governance of Novolica, with the support of her wealthy husband.

THE END

Milton Keynes UK
Ingram Content Group UK Ltd.
UKHW031046120324
439302UK00006B/542